# Ghostly Surprises

Lorna Shadow cozy ghost mystery - book 13

K.E. O'Connor

K.E. O'Connor Books

While every precaution has been taken in the preparation of this book, the publisher assumes no responsibility for errors or omissions, or for damages resulting from the use of the information contained herein.

All rights reserved.

No portion of this book may be reproduced in any form without written permission from the publisher or author, except as permitted by U.S. copyright law.

GHOSTLY SURPRISES

Copyright © 2022 by K.E. O'Connor

ISBN: 978-1-915378-46-0

Written by: K.E. O'Connor

# Chapter 1

Snow was banked on either side of Helen's little red car as we zoomed through the Berkshire countryside. The heating was on high, but I still wore my thick winter coat and gloves to keep out the chill.

"I can't believe we had this much snowfall overnight. It's so rare. I should invest in snow tires." Helen had to raise her voice so I could hear her over the Christmas tunes blasting from the stereo.

I gripped the door handle as the back wheels skidded on ice before the road straightened out in front of us. "Slow down! We're not late. Lady Drew isn't expecting us for another half hour. And I want to get there in one piece."

"I can't wait to arrive. Christmas is my favorite time of year, and we lucked out by getting this last-minute assignment to host an OMG sparkletastic Christmas party." She flipped her blonde hair back, revealing a pair of Christmas pudding earrings dangling from her lobes.

"I expect the personal assistant who broke her ankle doesn't think it was all that lucky. We got these jobs because of her accident." I opened the emails on my phone and re-read the message from the recruitment agency that arrived two days ago.

*Emergency! I'm in desperate need of an excellent event planner and caterer to oversee the Winter Wonderland Christmas Gala at the Drew estate. Double your usual rate guaranteed, and Flipper is welcome, too. Please, Lorna, I'm desperate. This is a long-standing client, and I can't let her down!!! I know you're not taking many assignments anymore, but think of all the Christmas goodies you can buy with the extra cash.*

When I'd seen how much Lady Kate Drew was offering for Helen and me to work for two weeks in the lead up to Christmas, I hadn't been able to turn down the job. Plus, I enjoyed Christmas. Although I didn't turn into a be-tinseled Christmas elf like my best friend, and terrible driver, Helen Holiday.

"Do you think we'll have any input into the finishing touches for the gala?" Helen said. "I've got so many ideas that I couldn't sleep last night."

"I doubt it." I reached back and scratched behind my dog's ears. Flipper was passed out in the back, as usual. He did it every time he went on a car journey. Next to him, snuggled up close, was Helen's feisty bald Chinese crested dog, Milly. "It's two weeks out, so everything has been planned. And when I spoke to the PA, Annie, she sounded organized. She kept apologizing for dropping us in it at the last minute."

"She's dropping us into tinsel heaven. And it was hardly her fault she fell off a ladder and broke her foot," Helen said. "Will Annie be around? I can run my ideas past her, see if she has any budget left for more sparkle."

"Annie's still working but only doing basic admin. It sounded like a bad break."

"With the extra money, we can treat everyone at Christmas and then take January off. Maybe we could try skiing again. Or..." She slid me a glance.

"Or what?" I gestured for Helen to watch the slippery road. The lane was getting narrower the deeper we went into the English countryside. "You want a vacation somewhere warm?"

"I wasn't thinking about a vacation. How about you spend January looking at venues for your wedding?"

"I'm not getting married yet." My hand tightened around the car door handle.

"Only because you won't fix a date with Zach. He keeps asking when he can make an honest woman of you, and you give him the brushoff. The guy will think you're not interested or you've changed your mind about marrying him."

"Zach knows I'm interested. I said yes to his proposal."

"Saying yes and setting a date are two different things. What's holding you back?" Helen barely eased off the gas as we zoomed around a blind bend.

I squeezed my eyes shut so I wouldn't see how close we were to the ditch. "I've been busy."

"We're all busy. You've got enough time to squeeze in venue hunting. Things get booked up years in advance. You don't want to miss out on your dream place."

I opened my eyes, relieved to see we were on a flat road, zooming past bare brown fields and hibernating trees overhanging the road. "We can have a ceremony in the backyard at home. Venue found."

Helen poked her tongue out. "No! Where's the fun in that?"

"It's less stressful."

"It's dull."

"I like dull."

"Impossible. You're best friends with me." Helen giggled. "It doesn't have to be a big wedding but at least hold it somewhere pretty."

"You're suggesting our yard is ugly?"

"I'm suggesting you're digging your heels in for no reason."

"I love Zach, and we have a great life together. Why change things?"

"Because he wants to marry you. What's the harm in that? And I desperately want to make your dress. I also want to make my own, so I can be the most stunning bridesmaid ever to walk up an aisle."

"I won't have an aisle if we marry in the backyard."

"There definitely won't be if you don't hurry and fix the date."

I settled back in my seat. Life had been busy. Although I wasn't working so much, I was part owner of a large house with Zach, Helen, and her husband, Gunner Booth, who was also Zach's brother. I kept myself busy around the house, took on freelance admin work now and again, and spent lots of time with Flipper. It was nice to take a break from my usual life.

Or should I say, my unusual life. I'd seen my fair share of ghosts over the years, mainly in the beautiful old houses I was sent to work in as an executive personal assistant. And although I helped them when they needed it, I didn't miss the freezing temperatures, icy fingers, nor the occasional blast of ectoplasm, or my fainting spells.

"Lorna, Zach's a patient man, but even his patience will run out. I know you don't like change, but this'll be a great change." Helen pursed her lips. "Although I don't see things changing much."

"Agreed. A ring on my finger changes nothing, so why bother?"

"Because it's romantic. Will you keep your last name like I did?"

"It would be strange to be called anything other than Lorna Shadow," I said. "Maybe Zach could become Mr. Zach Shadow."

"You could ask him. But neither of you will change your names if you don't get married soon."

Helen had a point. I didn't love change. It could be scary. And I was known for being stubborn and set in my ways. When I'd first met Zach, it almost broke us up several times. That and me always putting myself in danger when helping ghosts figure out how they died.

"We'll figure something out," I said. "Right now, we have our Winter Wonderland extravaganza to focus on."

"I'll be focused, but I won't forget your wedding." Helen drove on for another ten minutes as we both sang along to the festive tunes. "Oh, I see the house through the trees."

I peered through the ice-skimmed foliage and got a glimpse of the huge, detached pale cream mansion we'd be spending the next two weeks working and living in. A few minutes later, we discovered the gated entrance, and once through the gates, we headed along a winding gravel driveway.

"This is stunning," Helen said. "It'll look so beautiful when decorated. I'm surprised it's not sparkling and festive already."

"You always put up the Christmas decorations too soon."

"The first day in December is ideal. Then we get over a month to enjoy them."

"Gunner has tripped over that glowing reindeer by the fireplace three times."

"I keep telling him to be careful. His feet are too big, and Gunner never looks where he's going."

"That reindeer is huge."

"Hugely adorable."

"Just remember, we're not here to take over; we're here to oversee what's already been planned."

"Yes, mistress. Although I may make a few tweaks to the food if it's not festive enough," Helen said. "And when the dressers come to stage the decorations, I've got some ideas to run past them."

"Don't take over. You don't want to upset Annie."

"I won't get in her way. I'll be the soul of discretion. Just a nosy soul. Hey, that's a stunning fir tree in front of the house. It'll look beautiful covered in lights."

I repressed a groan and shook my head. Helen was the best friend a woman could ever want, four-legged fur babies not included, but she always went crazy over the top at Christmas. And then there was Easter, Valentines, Thanksgiving, and Halloween. Okay, she just loved an excuse to over-indulge on treats and dress up. That's kind of why I loved her.

A person dashed out in front of the car.

Helen squeaked and yanked the steering wheel to the left to avoid hitting them, and the car slid sideways on a patch of ice.

"Brake! You're going to hit that tree!"

Helen stamped on the brake, but the car continued to slide. "It's not responding."

The back of the car slid to the right, and I braced for impact as we collided with a tree.

The airbags deployed, and it took a few seconds before I could see what was going on. "Helen! Are you okay?"

She shoved down her airbag. "I think so. Where did that boy come from?"

"I have no idea." I checked the back seat. Flipper and Milly were awake and looking around, but seemed unconcerned, considering the car just crashed.

Once we'd deflated the airbags, we hopped out and checked to make sure the fuel line wasn't leaking and there was no fire risk.

Helen sighed as she looked at the dent in the side of the car and the deflating tire. "This is bad. I'm going to need my car. Why did that guy rush out of the trees? And where's he gone? We could be injured and need help. He just ran off."

I looked around, but the teenager I'd glimpsed for a second was nowhere to be seen. "He looked startled. Maybe he was being chased."

"Unless he was being chased by the abominable snowman who wants him for the festive pot, I'm not happy." Helen patted her damaged car. "At least we don't have far to walk."

"Are you okay?" A thin woman with gray hair dashed toward us from the direction of the road. "I was passing when I heard the bang. You hit a tree?"

"We did. Thanks for checking on us, but we're fine," I said. "Just shaken up. The car didn't make it through so well, though."

The woman looked around, her thin lips pursed. "Are you going to the Drew House?"

"That's right."

"For a visit?"

"No, we're working here for a couple of weeks." I tilted my head, waiting for her to introduce herself and explain her interest.

The woman shook her head and tutted. "You should leave while you have the chance."

"Leave? We've only just gotten here," Helen said. "We're working for the family until Christmas, organizing their Winter Wonderland extravaganza."

"Are you now?" The woman's eyebrows arched. "My advice to you is this, call a cab and go. Bad luck follows this family, and you don't want it attached to you."

"Bad luck?" I shivered as an icy wind cut through my thick, green winter coat. "What kind of bad luck?"

The woman glanced around and adjusted her red woolen hat. "I used to work here. I'm the former cook, Emma Smedley. And I'm paying the price because of the dark shadow cast across this household. It's not a nice place."

"I don't like the sound of that," Helen muttered to me.

"What dark shadow?" I said.

Emma's eyes widened. "You must know about Lord Albert Drew."

"No. We've only ever dealt with Lady Kate Drew. She hired us."

"Lady Kate." Emma sniffed. "She's part of the problem. I lost my job because of her."

"She didn't like your cooking?" Helen said.

"She doesn't like anything that has to do with the old ways. I suppose she'll be selling up soon and running off with the money."

"Why? Isn't she happy living here?" I said.

"I can't imagine she is. Who'd want to stay anywhere associated with such a tragic death?"

"Who died?" Helen almost whispered the question.

"Lord Albert. Six weeks ago. He had an allergic reaction to some nuts. Of course, the finger got pointed at me because I made the meals. But I knew about his allergies. I worked for the family for over thirty years. I'd never make a mistake like that."

"I'm sorry to hear he died," I said. "That must have been a shock for the family."

"It was a shock for me. I lost my job, and everyone thinks I'm incompetent. And the bad luck is affecting other people. Don't get me started on what happened to Annie Saunderson. Do you know her?"

"In a way. That's why we're here," I said. "We were hired because Annie injured her foot."

"She was injured because she was asked to do too much by Lady Muck. Annie was halfway up a ladder when she fell. It's not her job to scurry up and down ladders like some Victorian chimney sweep. She's in so much pain." Emma tightened the scarf around her neck and eyed the dark clouds overhead. "This place is cursed. Everyone gets injured or their lives ruined if they stay too long. Escape while you can. This place was lovely before Lady Kate got her Prada-clad toes under the table."

I glanced at Helen, uncertain what to do, and she shrugged at me.

"We're going to stay. Check things out for ourselves," I said.

"Your lives will be changed forever if you spend time in this house. No amount of money could convince me to return."

"You make it sound like the place is toxic."

"It ruined my life, killed Lord Albert, and injured Annie. How much more proof do you need? And Annie is such a kind woman." Emma's gaze drifted over us. "You seem like nice women, too, so I'm only telling you what I tell everyone else. Stay away from Drew House. The beautiful outside hides a rotten heart."

"Any more slanderous talk like that, Emma Smedley, and I'll have you arrested."

# Chapter 2

We turned to find a woman with ice blonde hair cut in tapered layers striding toward us. She was dressed in an elegant dark blue coat that stopped just below the knee and was belted around her tiny waist.

Emma's face blanched. She stepped back and bobbed her head. "I was just passing. I'm not doing anything wrong."

"You shouldn't be here," the woman snapped.

"I was checking to see if these ladies were hurt," Emma said. "I didn't mean any harm."

The blonde woman's gaze cut to the car. "There's been an accident?"

I stepped forward, noticing how Emma's demeanor had changed. She'd lowered her eyes, and her hands were clasped in front of her in a submissive pose. "We almost ran into someone. I'm Lorna Shadow, and this is Helen Holiday. The recruitment agency sent us."

"Oh! Of course." The woman's gaze cut from me to Helen, and her expression softened. "I'm Lady Kate Drew. It's a pleasure to meet you."

I glanced at Emma. No wonder she looked so cowed, since this was the woman who'd fired her. "Emma was checking to see if we were injured."

Lady Kate lifted her chin. "Very good. And were you?"

"No. We weren't going fast, but we got a surprise when a young man appeared out of nowhere. Helen had to swerve to avoid him."

"We wondered if he was running from something," Helen said. "He didn't stop to see if we were okay, so he must have been in a hurry."

"That's another one cursed by the house," Emma muttered.

"No more of your lies, Emma," Lady Kate said. "And I'll have a restraining order placed on you if you keep showing up uninvited. You won't be able to come anywhere near here. If you do, you'll go to jail. It's no less than you deserve."

"I don't want to be here, anyway." Emma's eyes narrowed, but she didn't look at Lady Kate.

"Yet I see you lurking around the gates most days."

"Because you owe me a month's wages. And you won't give me a reference. I need that money. It's almost Christmas. How can I buy presents for my family if I don't have my wage?"

"Find another job. One that doesn't let you anywhere near food," Lady Kate snapped.

"No one will employ me, since you've told the entire village I killed Lord Albert!"

Lady Kate sighed and turned away from Emma. "Excuse my former employee. And ignore everything she told you. If your car is still drivable, the garage is to the left of the house. You can leave it in there."

Helen studied the car. "If I take it slowly, I should be able to park safely. There's still some air in the damaged tire."

I inspected Emma and noticed her cheeks were pink and her lips pressed together. I was curious about what she meant by another person affected by the curse. Was the teenager we'd almost hit another one in trouble because of the Drew House misfortune?

"Emma, you need to leave," Lady Kate said. "Don't come back. And you won't be getting your wages. You should be grateful you're not in jail over Christmas."

"I did nothing wrong. The police have no evidence against me. You know I'd never hurt Lord Albert. He was a charming man and a lot kinder than you."

Lady Kate simply arched an eyebrow and pointed along the driveway.

Emma shot her a filthy look and scurried away.

"My apologies you had to witness that," Lady Kate said. "Emma is troubled. I wonder if it's because she's getting older. I'd have retired her years ago, but my late husband was far too tolerant of her poor behavior."

"I hope you don't think I'm prying, but did you really fire her because Lord Albert died?" I said.

Lady Kate nodded. "Please, deal with your car. Then I'll take you inside. It's getting cold out, and they're predicting more snow. I'll meet you at the front door." She turned and marched away.

"That was odd," Helen said. "Maybe we should turn back while we can. We don't want to get hit with any bad luck."

I looked at the broken car. "We're not going anywhere. Besides, you don't want to miss the fabulous Winter Wonderland extravaganza, do you?"

Helen peered at the house. "I really don't. But I don't want a curse to spoil our Christmas."

"There is no curse, just a few unfortunate things happening in a short amount of time."

"Are you sure?"

I was eighty percent sure. "Yes. Now, let's get this car moving."

We got into the car, and after a few goes, the engine coughed to life with an unhappy groan. Helen limped it slowly to the garage to avoid damaging the wheel too badly.

"Lady Kate and Emma clearly hate each other," she said.

"Let me see what I can find out about Lord Albert's death." I spent a moment scrolling through my phone until I found a few news articles. "All I'm seeing is information about an allergic reaction. There's no mention of any wrongdoing."

"It sounds like the police were involved, though," Helen said. "Emma mentioned them not finding any evidence to charge her, so it sounds as if she was under suspicion."

I continued to read an article I'd found. "The death was sudden after Lord Albert accidentally ate spiced Christmas nuts in his evening meal."

"Christmas nuts in November. He must have loved the festive season as much as I do." Helen turned off the engine as we reached the garage. "If he had an anaphylactic shock, there'd have been little anyone could have done. You know what I'm like when I eat oysters. I get a big puffy face and swollen lips from those slippery little suckers. All it takes is a tiny bite."

I grimaced. I couldn't understand the appeal of eating oysters. I was more of a dessert fan, which was handy, since Helen was as amazing in the kitchen as she was with a darning needle. "Lady Kate must have suspected Emma if she fired her."

"Maybe what Emma said was true. Lady Kate wanted to shake things up. She used her husband's death as a reason to do that. She may not have liked Emma's cooking. Some cooks get stuck in their ways, and their dishes get tired."

"Even so, I feel sorry for Emma. If she had nothing to do with Lord Albert's death, it sounds like she's lost everything."

We got out of the car, and I let Flipper out. He bounded about and sniffed around his new home. He was such an adaptable dog, and I took him everywhere. I called him my assistance dog, but he was much more than that. My ghost sensing ability had an unfortunate side effect of making me dizzy. I even fainted when a strong ghost was around. Flipper was a ghost sensing dog and always knew when a pesky spirit was creeping up on me and gave me a warning.

Helen scooped up Milly and tucked her into an oversized purse. Milly was an unofficial secret guest. Helen hated to leave her behind for long, so we were hopeful of hiding Milly while we worked. She was only small, so it might just work.

We headed to the front of the house. It was a beautiful cream stone detached mansion with four stories and a stunning view of the Berkshire countryside. I took a moment to enjoy the gorgeous ice-speckled fields and bare trees. Some people found winter gloomy, but I liked the stark beauty of the countryside.

Lady Kate was waiting for us by the front door. She gestured us inside. "I am sorry about your car. I'll make sure it's repaired at no cost to you."

"There's no need for that," I said. "The teenager who ran out in front of us should pay for the repairs."

"If we can ever find him," Helen said.

Lady Kate removed her gloves as she led us into a large circular entrance hall. "Well, I suspect that teenager was my son, Julian. He's... eccentric and spends a lot of time outdoors. Being inside makes him claustrophobic. Perhaps he heard your car, and it scared him. I told him you were coming, but he forgets things."

"We're friendly," Helen said. "I'm sure, when we meet Julian properly, we'll get along."

"I'm sure you will." Lady Kate smiled at us. "I'll speak to him and make sure he apologizes. And we have an excellent local mechanic. There's nothing he can't fix. Your car will be as good as new by the time you leave."

"Thanks. We'd appreciate that," I said.

"Would you like to unpack and settle into your rooms? Or I can show you around now, and we can discuss the work schedule."

"We're happy to get started," I said.

Lady Kate shrugged out of her coat. "Excellent. There's so much to deal with. The house dressers arrived this morning, and I'm not up to speed with everything Annie has planned. Not that I don't trust her. She does an excellent job, but I leave that kind of thing to her. I admit, I'm out of my depth."

"Is Annie around?" I followed Lady Kate as she led us along the hallway and into a huge dining room. There was a group of people unpacking boxes and a large, bare fir tree in one corner of the room.

"Yes, Annie's here," Lady Kate said. "We'll meet her shortly. Although I should warn you, she's on strong pain medication for her injury and has been dozing off at her desk. Not that I mind. I'm just grateful she's still able to work."

"You've picked such beautiful decorations." Helen was peering into a large crate. "Silver, green, and gold go so well together."

"You'll have to thank Annie for the color choices," Lady Kate said. "She's been dealing with everything to do with the party and the house dressing. Right this way, I'll show you the rest of the rooms on this floor, and then you're free to explore. Nowhere is out of bounds. Consider this your home."

Despite Emma warning us off, I was getting nothing but good vibes from the house and Lady Kate.

We spent the next twenty minutes walking around an exquisitely decorated house. The colors were classic greens and creams and the furniture expensive and antique.

We got to the kitchen, and I thought Helen was about to pass out with joy. It was a vast, open space with granite worktops and a large island in the center. Every kitchen gadget you could imagine was on display.

"The food for the party has been planned out," Lady Kate said to Helen. "But I'd appreciate it if you could take a look to make sure nothing is missing."

Helen half-bowed. "It would be my honor."

"There are caterers coming in for the evening party, so that's all in hand. But it needs coordinating. And, of course, you're welcome to add anything extra you think suitable."

Helen just about held in a squeak. "I can get started right away. And I'd love to get involved with the decorations, too. I have dozens of inspiration boards online."

"Most of that is in hand, but we do decorate the fir tree outside. I haven't given that much thought. My husband used to do it. You're welcome to take on that job, so long as it doesn't get in the way of your other duties."

"Consider it done. It'll be the most beautifully decorated Christmas tree you've ever seen."

"I'm sure it will. This way," Lady Kate said. "Annie should be in the office."

We walked into a large wood-paneled room with three desks and numerous cabinets and cupboards. Sitting behind one desk was a petite brunette in her mid-forties, wearing dark-framed glasses and a green suit.

"Annie Saunderson, I'd like you to meet Lorna Shadow and Helen Holiday," Lady Kate said.

Annie nodded at us both, a warm smile on her face. "I'm glad you're here. I've been panicking about not getting everything done in time." She gestured to her foot, which had a black orthopedic boot strapped around a white cast.

"We're happy to be here," I said.

"Annie is working shorter hours than usual," Lady Kate said. "She's not that mobile, so I thought it best we get extra help."

"I'm just about useless," Annie said. "I feel terrible for letting the family down."

"You haven't let us down," Lady Kate said. "Make sure you take your breaks. I don't want you suffering because of your accident."

"I promise, I will. And I need them. The drugs make me woozy." Annie yawned loudly. "I'm so sorry. I keep doing that. If I nod off at my desk, someone nudge me or waft strong coffee under my nose."

"We'll help out in any way you need us to. Nudges, coffee, reminders to take a rest," I said. "We've worked on plenty of events like this, and from what I've seen of your plans, you've done the hard work."

"There's still so much to get right, though. You know what it's like. We race around like crazy things until the last minute, when it all comes together and looks like it took no effort," Annie said.

"Annie, why don't you rest for an hour?" Lady Kate said. "I'll get Lorna and Helen up to speed as much as I can, and then you take over."

"Are you sure? I don't mind staying." Annie yawned again.

"I know you were here early this morning, and I don't want you overtaxing yourself. Especially since the doctor said you might need surgery."

Annie's mouth twisted to the side. "It's a possibility. I'm sure I'll be back on both feet as soon as I can."

"You won't be if you don't take a proper break. That's an order." Although Lady Kate's tone was fierce, there was a smile on her face.

"Then I'd better obey." Annie grabbed her crutches and stood carefully. "It's nice to meet you both. I look forward to working with you when I can keep my eyes open for more than ten minutes."

"We'll make sure this Christmas extravaganza is the best you've ever held at Drew House," Helen said.

"As long as it goes off with no major hiccups, that's all I hope for." Annie nodded at us, then limped out of the room.

Lady Kate eased the door shut behind her. "I feel awful about Annie's accident. She was helping me when it happened. I hate heights, and she offered to get some books I needed off the top shelf in the library. One minute, Annie was at the top of the ladder. I turned my back for a few seconds, and then she was on the floor."

"It's easy to overbalance if you're not careful," I said.

"The timing couldn't be worse. We always hold a Christmas gala every year. And Annie's been with us for years, so she knows how everything runs.

Given this year hasn't been the happiest, I wanted this event to be extra special."

"I'm sure we can pull it together between us. Try not to worry. We're experts at organization," I said.

"I'm grateful you could come at such short notice. Just be gentle with Annie. She feels guilty about not doing her full-time hours, and I don't want her stressed and pushing herself too hard." Lady Kate smoothed her hands over her hair. "So many troubles have come our way recently that, once we've gotten the festivities out of the way, I'm taking a well-earned break."

"Do you mean what happened to your husband?" I said, a little more bluntly than I should.

Lady Kate stiffened, and her smile faded.

"Emma mentioned it," I said hurriedly. "It's no wonder you want a break."

"It was a tragedy for us all. But my husband would have wanted this. He adored Christmas. Albert always began celebrating before Halloween. He'd get indulgent treats and sneak them out of the kitchen when he thought I wasn't watching." She shook her head, a sad smile on her face. "I considered cancelling the gala, but he'd have hated that. So, this year, the event will be in his memory."

"That's a wonderful thing to do," Helen said. "We'll make sure it's a perfect event to commemorate your husband."

I glanced around the room, half-expecting to see Lord Albert's ghost lurking in a corner. Since he loved Christmas so much, maybe he'd stick around for one more festive blowout. But there was no hint of a ghost, and Flipper was behaving normally, which suggested I had nothing to worry about.

I could only hope it remained that way.

# Chapter 3

After collecting our luggage from the car, Helen and I spent an hour unpacking our things. I was hanging the last of my clothes when Helen tapped on the bedroom door and walked in.

"Are you done? I thought we could have a quick look around on our own before we start work." She mooched to my dressing table and placed a sprig of plastic holly on the top.

"Almost. Where'd the holly come from?"

"I brought a bag of festive fun. I figured we could jolly up our rooms. You never know how people celebrate Christmas, so I didn't want to miss out on my usual sparkle." She poked her head into the attached bathroom. "You have marble, too. This place is impressive."

"It is. We're being spoiled."

"It is beautiful, but I love our home more," Helen said. "I was nosing around some of the other rooms, and the family has spared no expense. It's all very elegant. Milly likes it, too. I've set her little bed in the corner behind the hamper, and she's already asleep."

I shut the closet door. "Let's go see what the rest of the place is like."

We headed down the grand wooden staircase and into the office, where we'd be spending most of our time. I was immediately distracted by a whiteboard at the back that covered most of one wall. On it looked to be a neat, detailed plan of the Winter Wonderland Gala we'd be finishing planning.

I spent a few minutes looking it over, and everything made sense. There was a drinks reception, music and dancing, then a dinner, followed by a charity auction and then ice skating on a temporary rink.

"Annie knows what she's doing." Helen looked up from a file she was reading. "It's all detailed in here. We shouldn't have trouble keeping on top of this."

"I'm relieved. We've picked up a few last-minute jobs that have been unfinished messes. They're never fun. And I'm glad Annie is still around so we can ask questions."

Helen's phone buzzed with an incoming message, and she pulled it out and looked at it before texting back the sender.

I flicked through the file she'd been studying. There were schedules about the gala, when things were being delivered, and information about replies from the invitations sent out.

"Nearly everyone has replied to say they'll be attending," I said. "We'll have five hundred people here."

"Why wouldn't they want to come to an event in an amazing place like this?" Helen said. "And did you notice the dress code is winter white? It'll be stunning."

"We'd better stick to serving champagne and white wine to avoid any red wine accidents if things get excitable." I checked the drinks order and saw Annie had already thought about that.

Helen's phone buzzed again, and she replied to the message.

I pulled up a chair, grabbed a notepad and pen, and started a list of everything that still needed to be done. Flipper settled in next to me and curled in a circle on the floor, looking content as his eyes closed. If Flipper was happy, then so was I.

I glanced up at Helen. "Are you going to spend all afternoon texting, or could you give me a hand and look at the catering arrangements? That is your area of expertise."

"It's under control. I just need to be here to make sure the deliveries arrive on time, and then I get to order around the catering staff on the big day. It'll be fun being the boss."

"Don't forget, Lady Kate said you could order anything extra you like. Maybe you want to add a few special touches. Give the event some Helen sparkle."

Her eyes widened, and she grinned. "I could do a Winter Wonderland cake. I could make it in layers and have each one a different flavor. Then I'll cover it in white icing to make it look like snow. And of course, I'd add glitter, too." Before she elaborated on her ambitious cake plans, her phone buzzed again.

"Who are you talking to?" I said.

"Gunner." She texted him back. "You know what he's like. He misses me whenever I go away. The guy can't live without me."

"Sure, but he doesn't usually send you messages every ten minutes. Did you two have a fight, and he's making it up to you?"

"No! We never fight." Helen winked at me. "Well, only over his inability to put his socks in the hamper. That man can solve complex fraud cases, but ask him how to use the washing machine, and he plays dumb."

"So... if you're not making up, what are you talking about?"

"Christmas stuff. Gunner's terrible at telling me what he wants. I'm threatening to get him novelty underwear again if he doesn't make some serious suggestions."

I chuckled and shook my head. Last Christmas, Helen bought Gunner a pair of underpants with *Jingle Balls* written on them. They came with detachable gold tinsel.

Flipper lifted his head. He climbed to his paws and looked around the room before settling back down.

I petted his head. "Everything is fine. There's nothing to worry about."

"You don't think Lord Albert is haunting this place, do you?" Helen finally pulled up a chair and joined me at the desk.

"I've not gotten any sign of a single ghost." I set down my pen. "Which is unusual. Old places like this often have spirits wandering around."

"It's horrible what happened to Lord Albert. There he was, enjoying a good meal, when it was spoiled because of his allergies."

"I wonder if Emma did make an error. She added the nuts by mistake, thinking the dish was for another family member."

"I doubt she'd do that. Emma said she'd worked here a long time. And from experience, I know to be careful with people's allergies whenever I'm making them anything. I always get a list of things people can't eat, so I don't end up accidentally killing someone."

"As opposed to killing them deliberately?"

She elbowed me in the ribs. "You know what I mean."

Flipper stood again and walked to the door. He stared at it for a few seconds before returning to my side. He hadn't settled back down before he was up and wandering around the room.

This time, I followed him. I wanted to make sure there was nothing troubling him. I paused beside a large oil painting on the wall, showing Lord and Lady Drew. "Hey, take a look at this. I didn't know Lord Albert had been married before."

The picture showed a smiling man with a bright ginger beard. His paunch made him look a bit like Father Christmas. Next to him was a trim brunette with a warm smile and sparkling dark eyes. There was also a young girl in the picture.

Helen studied the painting. "Perhaps this is the original lady of the house."

"You must be right because here's Lady Kate with a small boy." I shifted to the next painting, instantly recognizing Lady Kate's graceful pose and stylish hair. "This could be the guy you almost hit, although he's much younger in this portrait. He must have arrived after Lord Albert remarried. I wonder who the girl is, though. Her name isn't on the picture's plaque."

Flipper ran to the door, just as a striking brunette in her mid-twenties skipped through it. "Daddy did remarry. And my stepmother is a monster."

We stared at her in surprise.

The young woman giggled. "Sorry, where are my manners? I should introduce myself before talking about my step monster. I'm Celeste Drew. That's me in the picture you were looking at."

"Nice to meet you, Celeste. I'm Lorna, and this is Helen. We're here to help with the Winter Wonderland Gala."

"Oh! Of course. After what happened to Annie, I thought it would be canceled. I'm glad you're here, though. I love a party." Celeste strolled around the room in a bright red floor-length dress, her silky dark hair tied in a ponytail. She kneeled and petted Flipper. "I like your dog. He's cute."

"He likes you, too," I said. "I hope you don't think we were being nosy, looking at the portraits. I was curious about the family."

"Not at all. Look away. I would if I was in a new place. I'd want to know everything about the people I worked for."

"You said your stepmother is a monster," Helen said. "What does she do to you?"

Celeste's nose wrinkled. "Kate's not nice. And I can tell she doesn't want me here. This is my home, too. Daddy wouldn't want me to leave."

"I'm sorry to hear about what happened to your dad," I said. "That must have been such a shock."

"Thank you. And it was." Celeste stood from petting Flipper. She walked to the portrait and looked up at it. "He was a kind man. Always smiling and laughing. The best father."

"We met Emma, the cook who worked here. She told us she lost her job over what happened," I said.

"Which was so unfair. Cook didn't do this to Daddy. She never had nuts in the kitchen. She didn't want to take the risk."

"No nuts at all?" Helen said.

"No. They weren't allowed. She was strict about it. Cook even told me off one day for bringing home some delicious fruit and nut chocolate. I had to eat it outside." Celeste chuckled. "She was funny like that, but I knew she was doing it to keep Daddy safe."

"His death was an accident, though?" I said.

"Oh, no. It wasn't. I'm certain Daddy was murdered."

My eyebrows flashed up, and I glanced at Helen, who looked as stunned as I felt.

"How do you know that?" I said.

"Because Cook was excellent at her job." Celeste patted her stomach. "And I had a bad feeling about that evening. I knew something terrible would happen. I didn't know to whom or what was going on, but I'd been feeling uneasy all day."

"You sensed your dad was going to die?"

"No, I can't predict the future. That's impossible." She giggled again. "Although that would be fun. I just knew the night would end in tragedy. I wish it hadn't been Daddy who'd died. After he passed, everything went wrong. The police came, everyone was miserable, and Kate fired Cook. My step monster barely shed a tear."

I stared at Helen with wide eyes. I had to keep asking questions to find out more about Lord Albert's death. If what Celeste said was true, and why would she lie, it was looking like it wasn't an accident.

"Do you think Lady Kate was involved with what happened to your dad?" I said.

"Yes! Well, I don't know for sure, but Kate didn't love him. I'm certain she only married him for his money. And now he's gone, she'll get it all. And she's doing her best to drive me out of the house." Celeste inspected the whiteboard and then drifted around the table. "And don't get me started on what she wants to do with my real mother. My step monster is a terrible person. I wouldn't put it past her to mix nuts into Daddy's food and sit there watching gleefully as he ate. She did nothing when he was struggling to breathe. She just sat there staring."

"I'm not sure I'd know what to do if someone choked in front of me," I said. "Lady Kate could have been in shock."

"I'd have tried the Heimlich maneuver," Helen said. "You know, when you stand behind someone and thump them. Although that wouldn't have helped your dad, since he was allergic to nuts."

"We may have saved him if we'd found an adrenaline pen, but the silly old thing forgot to say where he kept them. I was running around looking, while he was dying. Eventually, long after he was taken away, I found a pen in the back of his underwear drawer. Why keep it there?"

"He must have felt safe in his home," I said. "Especially if Emma forbade nuts in the house. He figured he wasn't at any risk of harm."

"Well, Daddy wasn't safe. Someone gave him those nuts because they wanted him dead." Celeste turned and looked around. "Is it me, or is it getting cold in here?"

Flipper ran around the room several times, his tail up as he sniffed the air.

"Yes, it is." My gaze darted around the room.

Helen glanced at me. "You don't think—"

"Oh, I see the reason." Celeste waved. "Hello, Daddy. These nice ladies are going to help me find out who killed you."

# Chapter 4

I stared at the spot Celeste was waving at and had to blink several times as the ghostly figure of Lord Albert Drew appeared. He had the distinctive orange beard and a smile just like the one in the portrait.

Helen grabbed my arm and leaned in close. "Is Celeste making this up, or can she really see her dad's ghost?"

"She's seeing something," I whispered. "She's looking right at him."

Flipper raced to the ghost and stood in front of him.

Lord Albert attempted to pet Flipper, but his hand passed through him, and Flipper whined and backed away.

"Um... Celeste, what are you seeing?" I said.

"Most likely, the same thing as you. It's my dad. He's here."

"You see ghosts?" Helen said.

"Sure. And I have a knack for sensing good in people. The second we met, I had a positive feeling about you and Lorna. You're special."

"Thanks," I said. "But you said we're going to help solve your dad's murder. Why would you think that?"

"Because I need help. I've never solved a murder before."

"And you think we have?" Helen looked at me and shrugged.

Celeste's appraising gaze slid over us. "I don't know you, but I know you'll help find out what happened to Daddy."

"We're organizers, not crime solvers," I said. "I do the admin, and Helen does the food."

"Don't forget the dress making," Helen whispered.

"Sure, and that."

Celeste waved away my comments. "I sensed you weren't only here to host the Winter Wonderland Gala. I have a sixth sense, you see. I've had it all my life."

Helen tilted her head. "A sixth sense? A ghost seeing sense?"

"Yes! Just like this cute dog," Celeste said. "You've all been sent to perform a Christmas miracle. Poor Daddy can't move on until we find his killer."

I moved closer to Celeste, trying to figure out how to let her down gently. "We're not—"

"This is amazing. You really can see your dad's ghost!" Helen said.

I shot her a warning look, not wanting her to give away all our secrets when it came to ghosts.

"It's a new thing, the ghost seeing bit, but I like it," Celeste said. "It makes me special."

"You haven't always been able to see them?" I asked.

"No, but I've always had odd feelings about things. And people. A couple of weeks after Daddy died, I knew something was wrong. My bedroom kept getting cold, and it felt like someone was watching me. Every time I looked around, there was no one there. I asked my step monster about it, but Kate said I was being childish. I even asked her if she believed in ghosts, and she threatened to put me into therapy."

"That's not kind," Helen said.

"Exactly! I told you she was horrible. Then, one night, I woke from a deep sleep. I don't know what startled me, but I fell out of bed and whacked my head on the bedside cabinet. After that, I could see Daddy. You see him, don't you, Lorna? So does your dog."

"Um... will I get fired if I say yes?"

"You'll get fired if you're not honest. And don't worry, I won't mention it to anyone. I quickly learned not to talk about spooky things. The rest of the family doesn't understand. This can be our secret. What a secret, though. Ghosts are real!"

Hearing Celeste's story reminded me of my introduction to ghosts. I hadn't been able to see them until I'd almost drowned. Maybe the injury Celeste got when she hit her head enabled her to see ghosts, too.

"You're able to talk to your dad?" I said.

"In a way. It didn't take me long to figure out we couldn't talk directly to each other. Well, I talk to him, but he can't reply. And I'm terrible at lip reading. So I've been teaching him to text. It's a slow process. He was hopeless using his phone when he was alive, but we've been able to communicate that way."

"That's clever," Helen said. "Lorna has the same trouble with ghosts."

I nudged her. I'd yet to admit I could see ghosts.

Celeste took Helen's comment in her stride. "The worst thing is, Daddy can't remember anything about how he died. I keep asking him questions, but we're stuck. Which is where you both come in."

Helen and Celeste looked at me. Lord Albert drifted closer, giving me a nod of encouragement. Even Flipper raised a paw, waiting to see if I'd admit to my unique skill.

I let out a breath. "That happens with ghosts. Especially if a person's death was sudden or traumatic. They block out the memories."

"Oh! How clever. That makes sense. After all, if you had a horrible death, you wouldn't want that as your last memory, would you?" Celeste said.

"Very true." I looked at Lord Albert, who'd been patiently hovering by his daughter's side while we talked. "It's nice to meet you. I wish it had been in different circumstances."

He nodded at me and smiled.

"I know you'll help us," Celeste said. "And we need it. It took me almost three weeks to get Daddy strong enough to use the phone to communicate. And he can only type a few words at a time. He doesn't have much energy, and I can't figure out how to keep him juiced up."

"Ghosts take energy from us and electrical items," I said. "He'd need to be around several people to maintain his strength. And I get the impression new ghosts don't know how things work. They drift around aimlessly unless they have someone to guide them."

"This is perfect. I knew you were ideal for this job. We're learning new things all the time, aren't we, Daddy?"

He nodded.

"This is my first ghost experience. It's exciting. Though I wish it wasn't my father I was communicating with." Celeste's bottom lip jutted out. "Maybe I can help other ghosts if I get good at it."

I nodded, although I was struggling to get my thoughts around meeting someone who could see ghosts as easily as I did. I'd previously met a ghost whisperer who saw dead animals and a couple of ghost sensitives, but this was on another level.

"So how will you solve Daddy's murder?" Celeste said.

"Um..." I looked at Helen for guidance.

"We have to help him," she muttered to me.

"Please!" Celeste gripped her hands together. "We can't have his ghost wandering about for eternity. How miserable would that be?"

"Horribly miserable." Helen elbowed me in the ribs.

"First, we need to find out if Lord Albert was actually murdered," I said. "Maybe it was an accident. You read about deaths from allergic reactions all the time."

"I'm sure he was. So is Daddy. And Cook didn't make a mistake." Celeste folded her arms over her chest. "Don't you agree, Daddy? You loved Cook, didn't you?"

He nodded slowly, his gaze drifting from me to Helen and back again.

"Loved as in more than a working relationship?" I said.

Celeste burst out laughing and doubled over, holding her sides. "Good one. No! Not romantically. Cook was sweet, but she's married. At least, she was. I'm not sure if her husband is dead, though."

"That doesn't always stop people from having a dalliance," Helen whispered in my ear.

Lord Albert was shaking his head, watching his daughter roar with laughter and smiling along with her.

"Shall we use a phone and see what your dad has to say?" I said.

Celeste pulled out her phone and opened it before setting it on the desk. "Of course. But I promise you, Cook and Daddy didn't have an affair. You know how to use this, Daddy. Take your time."

"Let me help," Helen said. "I'll watch what your Dad's typing and fill in the gaps." She moved to the desk so she could see the phone screen.

I gathered around it too with Celeste. "Lord Albert, do you agree with Celeste that you were killed?"

After about thirty seconds, the letter Y appeared.

"That must be a yes," Helen said.

Lord Albert nodded.

"And you agree with Celeste you don't think it was Emma who added nuts to your meal on the night you died?"

Another Y appeared.

"And he'd never voluntarily eat nuts," Celeste said.

Lord Albert nodded again.

"He loved his food, though. Daddy was a greedy guts. He was overindulging on early Christmas treats before the nut incident."

Lord Albert patted his belly and lifted his shoulders.

"So, if it wasn't an accident, and Emma didn't make an error, who do you think did it?" I said.

Lord Albert pointed at the picture, showing himself and Lady Kate.

"You think your wife killed you?" I said.

"Of course," Celeste said. "She's mean enough to do it."

"Have we just been hired by a killer?" Helen said.

"Let's not get ahead of ourselves," I said. "Lord Albert, when did you die?"

"It was two and a half months ago, at the beginning of November," Celeste said.

"And the police investigated?"

He nodded.

"They weren't much use, though. They asked questions, took a few pictures, but did little else," Celeste said. "They didn't seem interested. They kept calling it an accident."

"You don't think it was?" I asked Lord Albert. "Were there problems between you and Lady Kate?"

"She was spiteful and never let any of us have fun," Celeste said. "Kate wanted nothing to do with Daddy's old life."

Lord Albert nodded slowly, although he didn't look too happy.

"His old life?" I said.

"I'm a part of that old life," Celeste continued. "Kate changed things about the house when she moved in, and she was itching to get rid of me and anything connected to Daddy's happier days."

"It sounds like Lady Kate wanted a clean slate," Helen said.

"She was threatened by his old life. And having me around reminded Daddy how great things used to be. He regretted ever marrying Kate."

Lord Albert remained still, not agreeing or disagreeing. It would be good to get him on his own so we could have a balanced conversation without Celeste enthusiastically filling in the blanks.

"Do you think Lady Kate spiked your food with nuts?" I asked him.

Lord Albert looked at his daughter and shrugged.

"Is she the only person you can think of who might have done it?" I said.

He nodded, pointed at Celeste, and shook his head.

Okay, so Lord Albert didn't want his daughter to be a suspect.

"They didn't argue much, but they weren't a warm and cuddly couple. Not like Daddy was with my actual mom," Celeste said. "I never knew why they got divorced. It never made sense to me."

Lord Albert bent over the phone and slowly typed out the word *just*.

Helen tilted her head as she studied it. "Just bored? Just fancied a change? Just wanted a newer model?"

He shook his head at all her suggestions.

"Just got manipulated by a sly younger woman into giving up a lifetime of happiness?" Celeste said.

Lord Albert gave his daughter a reproachful look.

"I'm being honest, Daddy. Kate wasn't good for you. And she doesn't like me. That means I don't like her, either. I can only think badly about her because of the way she treats me."

"Did Lady Kate have an opportunity to put nuts in your dad's food?" I said.

"Oh, well, anything is possible." Celeste picked up the phone and adjusted the settings before placing it back down.

"You've said that before. What aren't you telling us?" I said.

She heaved out a sigh. "Kate never goes into the kitchen. She claims cooking is beneath her."

Helen harrumphed. "I think highly of someone who knows how to cook. Even just a few dishes. You never know when they'll come in handy. When I'm working in the kitchen, I create edible works of art. You should see my cakes. I was thinking of doing a special one for the Winter Wonderland Gala. Cooking isn't simple. And it's beneath no one."

I patted her on the arm. "You're an amazing cook."

"I expect your cakes are delicious. I hope you make one for the party. I'll have at least two slices.

Maybe three." Celeste grinned at her. "I make beans on toast. Does that count as a meal?"

"Not really. But full marks for the effort." Helen grumbled under her breath but seemed mollified.

"What did the police say about what happened to your dad?" I asked Celeste.

"They mainly focused on poor Cook and questioned her for several days. She was cleared of any involvement, but the finger of blame still points her way. And Kate added insult to injury by firing her. She marched her out the front door and told her never to show her face again. Cook has been in this family longer than I've been alive. I miss her. And she made the most amazing peach crumble and homemade vanilla ice cream. Kate doesn't like ice cream because she thinks it gives her spots. Helen, can you make ice cream and crumble?"

Helen grinned and nodded. "Of course."

"Excellent. I shall insist on having it every night. Ignore Kate if she tells you not to serve it."

"I'll make you a secret stash, and you can sneak into the kitchen and have some when no one is looking," Helen said.

"Even better. Then I don't have to share with my annoying little brother."

"Why were the police so interested in Emma?" I said.

"She was the obvious suspect. She had access to the food just before Daddy ate it."

"What was served that night?" Helen said.

"We had meatloaf and creamed potato. The nuts were in the meatloaf."

"Did the police question the rest of the family?" I said.

"Yes. I was questioned. My awful half-brother, Julian, was also questioned. So was Kate, Annie, and my mom."

"Your mom. Do you mean, Kate?" I said.

"Oh, no. My real mom. She lives here, too."

"She does? That's unusual. In this house?"

"Yes! It's not as if there isn't enough room," Celeste said. "Even though she's divorced from Daddy, they have a good relationship. Besides, I insisted they weren't allowed to part on bad terms. I was determined not to let Mommy leave. It took some convincing, but Daddy agreed she could stay. She's got a wing in the house, and I spend a lot of time with her. It's much nicer than the rest of this place. It hasn't been dolled up by Kate."

"What does Lady Kate think about your mom living here?" I said.

"If I was in her shoes, I wouldn't be happy," Helen said.

"I don't care what Kate thinks. This is our house, and I've been here longer than her. And she'd better not be thinking about selling. If she does, Mommy and I will be left out in the cold."

Lord Albert shook his head and jabbed at the letters on the phone, producing a jumble of nonsense words that made no sense.

"Don't be cross, Daddy. But I am worried. You had your head turned by Kate and look what happened to you. You've only been married a short time, and now you're dead."

"How long were they married?" I said.

"Only twelve years."

"Twelve years! And your mom has lived here ever since your dad married Lady Kate?"

"Of course. I stamped my foot, cried, and said I wouldn't sleep until Mommy was allowed to stay. They couldn't send her away."

"You must have been young when all this happened," Helen said.

"I was six. But I knew what I wanted. I even threatened to run away if Daddy didn't let her stay. So, I got my own way. Since then, Lady Kate has been horrible. You should meet Mommy, though. She's an angel." Celeste headed to the door then stopped. "Oh, I'm not sure she's back yet. Don't go anywhere. I'll see if I can find her. She can tell you about my hideous step monster and how she's ruined our lives."

Before I stopped Celeste, she dashed out of the room.

Lord Albert prodded the phone for a couple of minutes. *Sorry. Celeste excitable.*

"She's certainly headstrong," I said. "But now she's not here, I need to ask you, are you certain you were killed? It's easy to get your last few memories muddled. Perhaps all this talk of murder put thoughts in your head that shouldn't be there."

He shook his head and jabbed at the phone again. It took him a minute to spell out the word *killed*.

"This is an interesting twist on a murder mystery," Helen said. "You've got someone else who can see the ghost."

"And we have a way to communicate with him." I gestured at the phone.

"We are going to help Celeste and Lord Albert, aren't we?" Helen said.

"I don't think we have a choice. If we don't, Celeste will look into this mystery, anyway. And she's got her sights on only one person."

"The step monster."

I looked at the portraits. "Lord Albert and Celeste seem convinced Lady Kate was involved."

"How did she get the nuts into the food if she never goes in the kitchen?" Helen said.

"She snuck in when no one was watching. Or bribed the cook and then set her up. Or put them in the food when they were at the table. If Lady Kate caused a distraction, everyone's attention could have been on that. It would have been easy to slip a few nuts onto a plate."

"Which means we know it was murder, and we know what the murder weapon was. We just need a motive," Helen said.

"And as nice as Celeste seems to be, we have to include her on our suspect list."

Lord Albert jabbed at the phone, but only a garbled word came out. I didn't need to see his response. He didn't believe his daughter was involved.

"Should we have Lady Kate as our prime suspect?" Helen said.

Lord Albert nodded enthusiastically.

"She needs to be at the top of the list for now," I said. "But we've also got Celeste, her mom, Julian, and we should include Emma as well. Even though the police didn't find any evidence against her, that doesn't mean she's innocent. Clues can be missed, especially if the death was ruled an accident."

"And Emma was in the perfect position to add nuts to Lord Albert's food."

Lord Albert was shaking his head.

"Let's not rule out anyone for now," I said to him. "We'll do some asking around, see what we can learn about the night of your death, and take it from there."

Helen clapped her hands together. "How exciting. Not only do we have a huge Christmas extravaganza to sort out, but we also have a murder to solve. Best Christmas ever!"

I nodded, although I didn't share her enthusiasm. This job had just gotten a lot more complicated.

# Chapter 5

I was up early the next morning. After meeting Lord Albert and speaking to Celeste, we'd focused on work for the rest of the day so we could get on top of the Winter Wonderland Gala.

We hadn't been able to meet the first Lady Drew, though. Celeste had returned and let us know her mother was out for the day, so we'd arranged to meet her, along with the rest of the family, at breakfast.

Before I met everyone, I dressed in warm clothes, shrugged on a thick coat and pulled on a hat, and took Flipper out for his morning run. The grounds were pristine, with a fresh layer of snow covering the grass. It sparkled as the sunlight rose overhead, making everything look magical.

Flipper bounded around, kicking up snow and snapping at it. I threw a few snowballs for him to chase while I walked, enjoying the view.

He barked and raced to the trees. As I hurried after Flipper, I spotted a flash of movement and a glimpse of a pale face. Was that Lady Kate's son, Julian? Surely, he wouldn't be outside when it was so cold. If he was, he'd get frostbite. I'd only been out for fifteen minutes, and my nose was numb and my ears stinging with the cold, despite them being covered by a hat.

By the time I got to the trees, there was no sign of anyone. Maybe I'd mistaken the movement for a person, when it had been a deer or a rabbit, but I'd been sure I'd seen a face.

After giving Flipper a quick run, we headed inside. I dried him off in a big fluffy towel, got his breakfast, then freshened up before meeting Helen at the bottom of the stairs so we could eat together.

The table in the dining room had been laid for breakfast, and there was another table set out laden with food at one end. Standing alone at that table was a short, slender woman with a neat gray spiral of curls. She was dressed in pale pink silk.

"I reckon that's the first Lady Drew," Helen whispered to me.

The woman turned and slipped something into her pocket as her gaze met mine. She smiled. "You must be Lorna and Helen. I'm Mary Drew."

We walked over and joined her.

"It's nice to meet you, Lady Drew," I said.

"Mary is fine. Since I'm divorced, the title no longer seems relevant. And it's stuffy. Strip away the fancy names and jewels, and we're all the same underneath."

"Mary it is," I said.

"Celeste was telling me about you on the phone last night. My apologies I couldn't meet you on your first day, but I arrived back late and just about got myself into bed. I was so tired. Last-minute Christmas shopping, I don't recommend it." Mary chuckled, a wistful look on her narrow face. "Although I love the festive feeling you get browsing the stores and admiring all the beautiful decorations."

"I love Christmas shopping, too," Helen said. "Any shopping, actually. And I still have things to buy."

"I recommend a trip to Misty Vale. It's the nearest town to Drew House. It's well worth it, and we have some charming independent stores to explore." She gestured at the food.

"We'll be certain to make time for that." Helen picked up a plate and started inspecting under the tureens used to keep the food warm.

"And we weren't short on company," I said. "Celeste made us feel at home when we met her yesterday."

"My daughter's always enthusiastic when meeting new people. She loves to make people feel welcome. And we don't get many visitors. I love holding parties, and Albert loved them too, but, well, they don't happen much anymore." She gestured to the food again. "Please, help yourselves. I'm usually the first one down to breakfast. I like to get an early start. And I have the presents I bought yesterday to sort through and wrap. That'll take me most of the day."

I selected some delicious looking granola and a plate of fresh fruit. Helen went all in and dived into the festive cinnamon rolls with white icing.

"Would your dog like a treat?" Mary nodded at Flipper, who'd been patiently waiting by my side, his nose sniffing the delicious breakfast aromas.

Being a good boy, he hadn't made a move to grab anything.

"Flipper never says no to good food," I said.

He lifted a paw and wagged his tail, his gaze on a plate of sausages.

"He's a handsome boy." Mary petted his head.

"I hope you don't mind him being here. He's my assistance dog, so he goes everywhere with me."

"Of course not." She held out a small piece of sausage, which Flipper delicately took from her fingers.

"Shall we take a seat at the table?" Mary lifted her bowl of muesli. "Celeste said you wanted to talk to me about something important. Although I can't imagine what it could be."

I glanced at Helen, but she was focused on her food and trying not to drop anything off her full plate, which had three cinnamon rolls, a cranberry muffin, and a serving of mulberry spiced fruit jelly on it. "I'm not sure what Celeste told you about us."

"She tells me all kinds of fantastical things. My daughter has an extraordinary imagination." Mary settled in a seat and placed a white napkin on her lap. "She kept talking about Albert last night. She said you could help him."

I joined her at the table, and Helen sat next to me. "Did Celeste say how we might help your late husband?"

Mary regarded me steadily. "My dear, my daughter is unable to keep a secret. Although, I must admit, I was startled when she revealed she'd seen her father's ghost. Apparently, she believes you see him too, and you'll solve the mystery surrounding his death."

Helen choked on some cinnamon roll and took a large sip of her tea before she could speak. "Celeste really shares everything with you?"

"We've always been close. And after I separated from her father, I made sure we had a strong bond. I didn't want her to feel at a disadvantage because our marriage wasn't a success."

"That's good of you. Divorce can be difficult on children," I said. "What do you think of her suggestion about seeing Lord Albert's ghost?"

"I think I've overindulged my only child. But if it comforts her to believe in ghosts, and it doesn't harm anybody, I'm not going to suggest she stop talking about him." Mary pursed her lips. "Unlike Kate. She was less than kind when Celeste said she was seeing Albert floating around the house."

I shared a glance of surprise with Helen, who was so stunned by the conversation, she'd abandoned her food. "What do you think about the whole ghost situation?"

"I keep an open mind, but I prefer to see things with my own eyes before I believe them. And I've seen no signs of my late ex-husband floating around. And, to be honest, I'll be relieved if I never see such a thing. It would give me a fright." Mary took a small bite of muesli. "What about you? What are your thoughts on ghosts?"

"We keep an open mind, too," Helen said. "But if we can help find out what happened to Lord Albert, then we'd like to. Of course, we won't get in the way of any ongoing investigation."

"There is no investigation," Mary said. "The police asked some questions but ruled his death an accident. I expect Celeste told you our former cook, Emma, was questioned extensively. I felt sorry for the woman when the police kept prodding at her. She was a loyal employee, and if I had any power in this house, I'd have insisted she stay. But Kate was quick to dismiss her."

"Celeste mentioned Emma was a suspect," I said.

"Emma was ruled out. We all were. It's a puzzle what happened to Albert."

"If you don't mind me saying, your housing situation is unusual. After a divorce, you rarely find the couple still living together," I said.

Mary nodded slowly several times. "This is true. And I would have left if it weren't for Celeste. She was young when Albert requested a divorce and heartbroken we would no longer be together, so we compromised. I decided to remain here and be civil with Albert, which wasn't hard. Our marriage was good, and we hoped our separation wouldn't badly affect Celeste."

"You're comfortable living here?"

"I have been for the last decade or so. Although it was strange to begin with. And there were teething problems when Albert announced his plan to remarry." Mary set down her spoon and pushed her bowl away. "I'm not fond of Kate. I can certainly see the appeal, though, since she's an attractive younger woman. And I believe a man of Albert's standing is expected to upgrade his wife every ten years or so. It shows he's an attractive alpha male or something like that. I read a lot of women's psychology magazines. I sometimes think they make life unnecessarily complicated, though."

"If my husband upgraded me, he'd be missing vital parts of his body," Helen said.

Mary laughed lightly. "I'm sure with that threat looming over his head, he wouldn't dare. I don't have any hard feelings, and Albert was upfront with me about the marriage ending. We married young and too quickly, but we made a go of things for a while. And of course, we have Celeste, who's a delight."

"Other than Lord Albert's desire to upgrade, was there any other reason you separated?" I asked.

"We fell out of love with each other. The marriage became more of a friendship, and we realized things weren't quite right long before the divorce." Mary let out a gentle sigh. "In truth, I think Albert had his arm twisted by his friends. He said he wanted passion back in his life. I wondered if he was having a midlife crisis. Although the expensive sports car never showed up, the younger wife did."

"You don't mind talking about your split?" I said.

Mary waved a hand in the air. "Forgive me. I'm rambling to strangers, but I spend a lot of time on my own. Kate discourages me from having friends over, so I keep my own company. It's wonderful to talk to people who aren't judging me. And I don't mean to sound bitter. I'm really not. I cared for Albert as a friend, and we adjusted to this living situation. He also generously gifted me an entire wing of the house, so I have everything I need. I don't even have to come here to eat, but Celeste likes to see me for meals, so I make the effort. And sometimes, it can be an effort if Kate is in a bad mood. Which happens a lot."

"Was she often moody with Lord Albert?"

"Now and again. Nothing serious, though. At least, not that I witnessed."

"What do you think about Celeste's insistence her dad's death wasn't an accident?" I was surprised Mary was being so open, but she seemed to share her daughter's trait of concealing nothing.

"I'm skeptical. But it is strange those nuts got into Albert's dinner. We all knew about his allergy and had to be so careful. I even stopped using a certain type of body butter because the smell would set off his allergies. I can't think how they got into his food."

"They could have been added during the preparation," Helen said.

"It's possible. Although I'm certain it wasn't Emma's fault. When we hired her, we were clear about the issue around nuts, and she was always happy to help. She'd frequently consult over the menus to make sure there were no other allergens or issues she needed to know about. She was good like that."

"If it wasn't an accident, how did they get in there?" I said.

"No one knows. The police investigated and questioned everyone, including me, but I couldn't tell them anything. And that evening, I wasn't feeling well. I'd had a headache most of the day, so I got a simple meal and left the dining room to eat alone. I thought an early night might help my head. The first thing I knew about Albert was when the ambulance arrived. I couldn't believe it when I got to the dining room, and he'd gone." She lifted her napkin and dabbed the corner of her right eye. "He must have gotten lax about keeping his medication close."

"Were you ever worried about Lord Albert's safety? You didn't think someone was out to get him?" I said.

"Oh, no, nothing like that. When we were married, I always kept a supply of first aid bits close to hand to deal with scrapes and bruises. Maybe it's a thing a mother does. And I always made sure Albert's EpiPen was included, just in case." Mary's hand shook a little as she folded her napkin. "Celeste was devastated. Of course she would be. She'd always been close to her father. It's why I'm even more grateful I stayed here. If I'd moved away after the divorce, she'd have been on her own, with no support."

"Not even from Lady Kate?" Helen said. "After all, she is her stepmother."

"I expect you've heard Celeste call her the step monster. She even does it to Kate's face." Mary shook her head. "I've told her off about it, but she insists it's an accurate description. There's no fondness between them. Kate tolerated Celeste while Albert was around, but since he's been gone, she's become frosty toward both of us. I suspect it's only a matter of time before she orders us to leave."

"Can she do that if Lord Albert gave you part of the house?" I said.

"Ah, you see, that's the tricky thing. It was an unofficial gift. Nothing was put in writing.

And Albert left everything to his current wife. Unfortunately, that's not me."

"It all went to Lady Kate?" Helen said.

"Albert provided a trust for Celeste and his son, by Kate, Julian. I was gifted a cottage on the Cornish coast. We used to go there for summer vacations years ago. It's a beautiful place but remote. If I moved there, I'd barely see Celeste. I don't drive and dislike public transport. I could hire a driver, but it's the expense, you see. Albert didn't leave me any funds of my own."

"Perhaps Celeste would move with you," I said. "She may have had enough of living here if things are difficult with Lady Kate."

"It's unlikely. Celeste loves this house. She grew up here, so it's all she knows. I'd feel guilty dragging her away. Besides, she's an independent young woman. As much as I'd like to, I can't keep her with me forever." Mary sipped her coffee, her intelligent gaze moving from me to Helen. "Neither of you seemed surprised when we discussed Albert's ghost."

"As Helen said, we keep an open mind about everything," I said.

"That's a good mindset to have. Some people would leave the second they heard about a haunting. Especially if it was associated with a suspicious death."

"We've worked in plenty of suspicious places." Helen laughed, and her cheeks glowed pink. "I mean, we've worked in places where suspicious things have gone on. No! I didn't mean that, either. I..." She looked at me for help.

"We're happy to stay. And both of us have worked in old houses, even a few castles. They all creak and groan, making it easy to believe they're haunted."

"I'm glad you're both here. Celeste needs companions, so I hope you won't mind indulging her with her ghostly pondering."

"Not at all. Celeste seems like a lot of fun," I said.

"She is, but she's naïve. I blame myself. I've kept her sheltered. The world is tricky to navigate and don't get me started on social media. It's enough to make your eyes bleed, some of the things I've seen. I'm sure she'll appreciate having older role models." Mary chuckled lightly. "Excuse me, not that I mean either of you is old. You appear to be beautiful, intelligent women. But Celeste spends too much time with me, and I'm set in my ways. I don't want to hold her back when she has the world at her feet. I also don't want her worrying too much about what happened to her father. It may simply be a mystery that's never solved."

"Well, if we can help solve that mystery, we'll do it," I said. "Whether there's a ghost living here, or it's a case of creaky floors and rattling pipes, it sounds like Celeste could do with a friend."

Mary clasped her hands together. "That's good of you, and I'd appreciate that. I'll find you both a little Christmas gift as a thank you for taking Celeste under your wing while you're here."

"There's no need. We're happy to help."

Voices approached the room, and a moment later, Lady Kate, Celeste, Annie, and a young man I didn't recognize entered. His head was down, and he was shuffling his feet across the carpet as if they were too heavy to pick up.

Celeste dashed over and hugged her mom before grinning at me and Helen. "I delayed everyone for as long as I could so you could talk in secret about you know what."

"There was no need for that, my dear," Mary said, her smile indulgent as she shook her head at her daughter. "Get yourself some breakfast."

Celeste dashed to the table, spent a few minutes helping Annie load a plate as she struggled to balance everything, and then sorted through the cranberry croissants.

Lady Kate poured herself a black coffee and settled in the seat at the head of the table. She nodded at me and Helen. "I hope you had a pleasant first night."

"Yes, thanks. The bedrooms are comfortable," I said.

"Perfect," Helen said. "I slept like a Christmas yule log."

"Excellent. And I see you've met Mary. I thought you were planning to go away this weekend?" Lady Kate's tone cooled as her gaze flicked over Mary.

"I had a change of plans." Mary focused on her muesli.

"I wish you'd tell me when you change things. I was planning to invite friends to stay."

"They can still visit. I won't get in your way."

"But it'll be awkward, with you lurking in the background, like the marital ghost of Christmas past and best forgotten."

Helen's eyebrows shot up, and she turned her head my way.

Mary sat up straight in her seat. "I never lurk."

"You know what I mean. People think it's strange you're here. How are the renovations going on the Cornish cottage?"

"They're still ongoing," Mary said. "They won't be ready until at least March of next year. The builders want to down tools early so they can enjoy the festive period. I said that was fine. Everyone deserves a break this time of year."

"I'm sure if you paid them more, they'd keep working, then you'd be able to move out sooner and celebrate Christmas in your new home, rather than your old one." Lady Kate sipped her coffee.

"Mommy's not going anywhere." Celeste hurried to the table with a plate of croissants and half a melon cut into chunks. She set the food down, then dashed back and grabbed Annie's plate before joining us at the table. "We're happy here. I refuse to have Christmas anywhere else."

"Wouldn't you like to live somewhere else and make new traditions?" Lady Kate said. "And your father so generously gifted the cottage to your mother. You can spend a couple of years down in the southwest and enjoy the beaches in the warm weather."

Celeste slapped her hand on the table. "You can't throw us out. This is our home. Daddy will hate you if you try."

"Child, your father has no say over matters involving this household anymore."

"Annie, tell her she's wrong." Celeste gestured at Lady Kate. "You knew Daddy as well as anyone. He wants us here. Tell her!"

Annie hobbled over on her crutches. She nodded a greeting at me and Helen before struggling into her seat. "Maybe a new scene is just what you need. And Cornwall is beautiful."

Celeste tutted. "You're no help."

I glanced at the teenage boy. He was dark-eyed and pale-haired and had a dash of hormonal acne on his chin. He was lurking by the food, grabbing bits now and again and stuffing them into his mouth. His gaze kept flicking to the window as though he was thinking about diving through it.

"Why don't you take the cottage, Kate, and we'll stay here?" Celeste said, her tone shifting to sickly sweet in a flash. "I'm sure Daddy made a mistake. After all, there's only one of you. We need more room."

"There's also Julian," Lady Kate said. "He loathes change. Your father's wishes were clear. This house is mine."

"We're not going anywhere so close to Christmas," Celeste said. "This is Daddy's favorite time of year. He wants us here."

Lady Kate let out a sigh. "Please stop talking about him as if he's still alive. It's distressing."

"But..." Celeste looked at me.

I lifted a shoulder and shook my head. There was no way I was losing this job, even if it meant I had to conceal the truth about Lord Albert's ghost. I hoped Celeste didn't feel I was letting her down.

Lady Kate slowly set down her cup. "This should be your last Christmas here. The New Year brings change, and a fresh start for both of you would be ideal. We need to move on from this tragedy."

A swirl of icy air spun around me, and a second later, Lord Albert appeared. He was glaring at Lady Kate and shaking his head.

"Uh-oh," Helen muttered as she leaned close. "Have we got ghostly company?"

"Daddy!" Celeste jumped from her seat. "Now you're in trouble. He's here, and he's not happy with you, Kate." She jabbed a finger at Lady Kate. "You always cause problems for us."

Lord Albert spun around the room, stopping by Lady Kate's chair and shaking his head again before shooting away.

She rubbed her arms briskly. "We need the fires lit in the morning. I hoped the new heating system would be more effective, but I've just got such a chill down my back."

Flipper jumped up from where he'd been nestled by my feet, hoping to get treats from the breakfast table. He chased after Lord Albert, snapping at his heels as he tried to get the ghost to behave.

"Lorna, what's wrong with your dog?" Lady Kate said. "I thought he was trained. Surely an assistance dog shouldn't do that. He looks like he's chasing a fly."

"A noise unnerved him," I said. "He'll be fine in a moment. Flipper, get over here."

Flipper kept chasing Lord Albert, who zipped through the wall, leaving Flipper barking at nothing.

"It's your fault he's barking," Celeste said to Lady Kate. "You make everyone angry. You've upset Daddy and this nice dog."

"I did no such thing," Lady Kate said. "Lorna, if your dog can't behave, he'll have to go outside. He can stay in the stables."

"He'll behave. Sometimes, he takes a day to settle into a new place." I recalled Flipper, and he sat by my side on alert, staring at the wall.

"Flipper was chasing Daddy," Celeste said, "who is unhappy with your plans to throw me and Mommy out on Christmas Day."

"Celeste, that's enough!" Lady Kate said. "Albert is dead. He's not coming back. You need to accept that. Every shadow isn't your father creeping out of the grave. It's morbid the way you obsess about him. It upsets me."

"Perhaps we should leave." I pushed back my chair and nudged Helen, who'd been avidly following the bickering like it was her favorite TV medical drama. I was keen to hear the row, too, but I had to talk to Lord Albert. He couldn't chase around rooms and unsettle people, especially not if Celeste was going to point him out every time he appeared.

"Good idea." Helen stuffed the last of her croissant into her mouth.

"Now look what you've done," Celeste said. "You've upset Lorna, Helen, Flipper, and Daddy. Everyone hates you."

Lady Kate simply sighed, picked up her coffee, and left the table to stand by the window.

I hurried out of the room to find Lord Albert whizzing back and forth along the hallway. I dashed over and stood in front of him, holding up a hand like an emergency stop signal. "Lord Albert! You can't do that. It's not fair on anyone. You're upsetting your family, and you're getting Celeste overexcited."

He pointed at the room we'd just left and then at his chest.

"We will investigate what happened to you, but we need to do it discreetly. You rattling tables and making everything freezing isn't discreet."

He gestured to my pocket, and I took out my phone and opened the messaging app.

I glanced over my shoulder. "Helen, you and Flipper keep guard. Make sure no one comes out and sees what I'm doing."

"I'm on it. Come on, Flipper." She snuck back to the dining room door with Flipper and stuck her ear against it. "They're still arguing, so we're good."

It took a few minutes and several false starts before Lord Albert typed out what he wanted to tell me. *Promise you will help.*

"Of course. But on one condition. No more scaring your family. After all, it's nearly Christmas. This is the season of goodwill, not spooking people like it's Halloween." I arched an eyebrow at him. "You need to stay calm and be patient."

He didn't look happy about my suggestion, but finally nodded.

"Perfect. Then you relax, and we'll get started on finding out how those nuts got into your last meal."

"Is everything good with Lord Albert?" Helen whispered.

"It is. We need to get to work on figuring out this mystery, though."

"Where shall we begin? Celeste isn't a fan of Lady Kate, and she seems spiky. Is Lady Kate still our prime suspect?"

"I think so, but we should visit Emma first. Let's see why the police considered her the most likely to have killed Lord Albert."

# Chapter 6

After our lively breakfast encounter with the family, I'd retreated to the office with Helen, and we'd spent a day working through the remaining tasks and setting up a plan of action for the Winter Wonderland Gala.

Snow had been lightly falling all day, and it looked like we were inside a giant snow globe as I took a break and stared out the window. It was late afternoon and already getting dark. Piles of snow were banked up on either side of the driveway where it had been cleared.

"I thought you might need this." Helen walked in with a tray in her hands. There were two mugs of steaming hot chocolate sprinkled with pumpkin spice and a plate of iced Christmas cookies in the shape of snowmen. She had her purse over her arm and Milly's head poking out of it.

"I'll spoil my dinner, but I can never resist your baking." I took the mug of hot chocolate and grabbed a couple of cookies.

"So it gets spoiled by delicious treats. Perhaps we don't want to go to dinner if every meal with the family is like breakfast." Helen settled in a chair, set

Milly on her lap, and dunked a cookie into her hot chocolate before sucking off the icing.

"I feel sorry for all of them. It's a tricky situation to be in. I understand why Mary wants to stay, so she can remain close to Celeste, but if everyone's always fighting, it must be stressful."

"Did you see Julian lurking about? At least, I think it was Julian. No one made the introductions. He could barely look anyone in the eye and seemed desperate to escape." Helen arched an eyebrow. "I noticed he didn't apologize for damaging my car."

"It was the ditch and tree you hit that damaged the car, but I get your point." I nibbled the edge of my cookie, then copied Helen and dunked it in the hot chocolate. "Maybe Mary and Lord Albert thought they were doing the right thing by staying under the same roof, but I don't think it helped Celeste or Julian."

"I agree. Children know when there's trouble in a relationship. Celeste does seem naïve, and as for Julian, from what little we've seen of him, he's unhappy."

"Maybe we should gently nudge Mary about the move to Cornwall once this is over," I said.

"I can think of worse places to move to. And if there's already a house there, it would be better for everyone if they parted ways." Helen licked icing off her fingers and then held one out for Milly to explore with her small pink tongue. "Lady Kate could have been kinder when suggesting Mary and Celeste leave, but the change might be what everyone needs. They can start afresh. We solve the murder, move people on, and everyone is happy or, at least, less miserable and argumentative."

"What if Mary and Celeste don't want to go? After all, this place must be worth a fortune. And I suspect Lord Albert left behind plenty of money. If they move, it's as good as admitting defeat and accepting they won't get anything."

"Money is a strong motive for murder," Helen said.

"Celeste and Julian have trust funds. If they're generous, money wouldn't have been a motive for them."

"It could have been a motive for the wives." Helen munched on another cookie as I turned to look at the large whiteboard we'd been updating all day. I loved to make a plan. I did it with all my work and was the same when helping a ghost. If you failed to plan, you planned to fail. It was a motto I lived by.

I picked up a red marker pen and ticked several things off the board we'd completed that day as I mulled over the motive.

"Shall I put up a new blank board, so we can create a to-do list for how to solve Lord Albert's death?" Helen giggled at me.

I turned and saw the grin on her face. She knew me too well. "Let's go visit Emma, later. The police were interested in her, and it would have been easy for her to slip nuts into the food."

"And if it wasn't Emma, she could be a font of information since she worked here for so long. She might give us insider tips about who to target as a suspect." Helen was finishing her hot chocolate when her phone rang. She checked the caller. "I'll be back in a minute." She answered it and hurried out of the room, taking Milly with her.

While I was waiting for her to come back, I called Zach to see how he was getting on, but his line was engaged. So I called Gunner, instead. He usually knew where Zach was since we lived together.

"Hey, Lorna. How are things at the fancy house? Gotten into any trouble yet?"

"So far, so good. How about you? Have you figured out what you're buying Helen for Christmas?"

He groaned. "Don't remind me. She keeps sending me links to things on her wish list. There are dozens of things to choose from, including furry slippers with tiny pom-poms and designer sweaters. I mean, I'm sure it'll all be great, but who needs so much stuff?"

"You know Helen. She loves her clothing. And don't forget the shoes."

"I was thinking of getting her an experience. Something we could do together. Making memories is more important than another designer sweater. How angry would she be if I took her wild camping for a long weekend?"

"We are talking about the same Helen, aren't we? The Helen who does her hair perfectly, has gleaming nails, and prefers high heels to pumps."

He chuckled. "I know. She'll yell at me for a week, but it would be amazing. We can have a campfire and cook outdoors. Then sleep under the stars and go trekking during the day. And I've already gotten Milly a Christmas present that'll fit with the hiking plan."

"What did you get her?"

"A dog papoose."

"That's a thing?"

"Sure. Loads of people take their cats and dogs with them when they go camping. Of course, the ones with little legs can't walk long distances, so they strap them in a papoose and off they go. They love it."

"Gunner, I admire you for thinking outside the box, but it's an awful idea. If you want to take Helen away somewhere she'll enjoy, pick a luxury hotel that accepts pets. Somewhere she can be pampered."

"But she pampers herself all the time. What about trying something different?"

"The only mud she wants to get near is from a face pack. Stick to her wish list items rather than go out on a limb. Unless you're angling for divorce papers as a gift."

"Helen is adaptable. After all, you two are always heading off to new places and having to fit in. You're doing that right now."

"Adapting to life in an enormous mansion with an all you can eat breakfast and staff is different to slumming it under the stars. I mean, I wouldn't mind doing that with Zach and Flipper, but with Helen, it wouldn't work."

"I'll look into it some more," Gunner said. "I could always pack some of those mask things in my rucksack. Helen can star gaze and have a face pack at the same time."

I winced. "Good luck. How's Zach doing? I just called him, but he's on the line with someone else."

"He's good. Not busy at work, since there's less gardening this time of year. He's been doing some of the jobs on his honey-do list."

"I didn't leave him a honey-do list."

Gunner chuckled. "Yeah, but Helen left me one. I suggested Zach take a look if he got bored. And you know what Zach's like. He has to keep busy. He put up the shelves in the study yesterday. They look good. If I'd done them, they'd have been wonky."

"When he's finished his call, ask him to ring me. I've got a few ideas about Christmas I want to talk to him about."

"Will do. See you both soon."

Just as I ended the call, Helen walked back into the room with Milly tucked inside her sweater.

"Hey. Who was your call from?" I said.

"Gunner. He has to hear my voice every day, or his life isn't worth living. It's so hard having a guy that obsessed with you."

I stared at her and narrowed my eyes. "You were talking to Gunner? Just a minute ago? That was who called you?"

She nodded. "Of course. He was saying how much he missed me."

I wanted to keep quizzing Helen but didn't know what to say. I'd caught her out on a lie. Why would she say she'd been speaking to Gunner when that wasn't possible?

"Shall we finish up here and then go?" she said. "We can head over and see Emma before dinner. I checked with Lady Kate when I finished my call. We can use a family car to get around while the repairs are being done on mine."

I nodded slowly, still puzzling through why she hadn't been truthful with me. "Sure. Give me half an hour. Do you have Emma's address?"

"Yep. I got it from Celeste. I'm super organized." Helen cocked her head. "Is everything okay?"

"Yeah. Everything is great."

"If you're worrying about Lord Albert, you don't need to. We'll find out what happened to him. You always figure out these mysteries. No one can keep a secret from you for long." Helen walked to the door. "I'll settle Milly down, then find the keys for the car and meet you outside. Shall I take Flipper to keep Milly company while we're out?"

"Sure. Good idea. I'll see you out there." I watched her go, the cookies sitting heavily in my stomach. I picked up my phone, meaning to call Gunner again and double check if he'd been speaking to Helen before me, but that made little sense. I'd called him after Helen had taken the call that was supposed to be from him.

I set down my phone. Helen wouldn't be fooling around on Gunner. They adored each other. And although occasionally their interests clashed, they made it work. There must be another reason Helen wasn't being truthful, but I couldn't figure out what it was.

Forty minutes later, we were zooming along the icy country lanes toward the enchanting sounding town of Misty Vale. I kept giving Helen the side eye as I struggled to figure out why she'd lied about her conversation with Gunner. Were they planning a Christmas surprise for me? If so, I wasn't a big fan of surprises, and Helen knew that.

Her overly enthusiastic speeding distracted me from my musings. "They don't grit the roads around here. Slow down! Or we'll be the next ghosts that need help."

Helen eased off the gas a fraction. "I don't want to be too long. We might miss something important at dinner tonight."

"Earlier, you weren't keen on spending another meal with the family."

"I'm not. All that bickering gives me a headache, but they could reveal something useful that's connected to Lord Albert."

I really didn't want another tense dinner to deal with. "We could eat out. And you mentioned you had Christmas shopping to do. Do you need to get something for me?"

"Noooo. You're sorted."

"Gunner?"

"His gifts are sorted, although not his main present. Although I'm doing him a Christmas stocking this year. I'm filling it with fun bits to keep him entertained. You know how grumpy he gets if he isn't working. You should do the same for Zach."

"He's a bit old for a Christmas stocking."

"I don't care if he's five or a hundred and five. Everyone deserves a stocking from Santa."

The GPS directed us ten miles from the Drew house, and we stopped outside a tiny mid-terraced cottage with a tired-looking front door.

"This is Emma's place." Helen climbed out of the car. "Let's go see what she has to say for herself."

We had to knock for almost a minute before Emma opened the door.

She didn't hide her surprise at seeing us. "Huh! You two are still around? You didn't take my advice about escaping the bad luck?"

"No, we're sticking with our jobs for now," I said.

"It would be nice to have one of those." Emma regarded us with suspicion.

"We have a few questions for you, if you can spare the time."

"You want to know about your awful new boss, I suppose."

"Well, yes. But not just about Lady Kate. Do you have a few minutes to talk?"

"I'm not doing much else. You'd better come in. But you shouldn't be out for long. More snow is predicted." Emma ushered us into a low-ceilinged front room. There was a cozy fire burning in the hearth and a comfortable-looking beige couch along one wall. She led us into the next room, which was a small kitchen with a sloping floor, and set a kettle on the stove.

"This is a cute place," Helen said.

"It's not much, but it's home. At least for now. So, what can I do for you?"

"Lord Albert," I said. "You must have gotten to know him well over the years."

"As well as an employee can know her boss. But I reckon I knew him better than most. He wasn't one of those fancy types with airs and graces. Not like the second wife. He always had a kind word for me and made sure I got a Christmas bonus. Of course, that won't be happening now."

"You're still not getting anywhere with Lady Kate giving you your wages?" I said.

"She's not moving. I've even threatened to sue her, but it was a hollow threat. I've got no money to take her to court." Emma heaved out a sigh. "I don't know what I'm going to do about Christmas gifts. I was relying on that money."

"Perhaps she'll change her mind," Helen said. "Especially if we figure out what really happened to Lord Albert."

I nudged her with the tip of my boot. This was supposed to be a discreet line of questioning.

She shrugged her apology.

Emma pursed her lips and gave Helen the once over with a sharp look. "How do you think you'll do that? You can hardly summon him for a chat. I wish you could. Then he'd tell you what happened and prove my innocence."

"That would be an extraordinary thing. Talking to the dead." Helen grinned at me. "We're curious to learn about what happened to him."

"Why? What's it to you?"

"The household has been unsettled by his death," I said. "It doesn't make it a comfortable place to work."

"And it would be wonderful if they could all get closure. You included," Helen said. "Then you can celebrate Christmas without having anything to worry about. You may even get your job back."

"I can't see that happening. And I'm not certain I'd want to work under Lady Kate."

"You don't miss it?" I said.

Emma turned away. "Sometimes. And it would be good to have this cleared up. But if you're here to ask if I had anything to do with it, you can leave. I'm innocent, and that's been proven. And pay no mind to what Lady Kate tells you. I'm honest as the day is long. I worked hard for that family. I planned to spend the rest of my working days there. Of course, that won't happen now. And if I don't find another job soon, I'll get behind on the rent for this place."

"You don't want to lose your home," I said.

"Of course not! And I'm too old and set in my ways to start again somewhere new."

"Maybe we can help," I said. "And wouldn't it be great if we could figure out what happened to Lord Albert and prove you had nothing to do with it?"

"How will you do that?"

"We've asked around, and it seems several people think his death wasn't an accident," Helen said.

"I agree with those people." Emma dumped loose tea into a chipped brown teapot and poured in boiling water. She set the lid on the pot. "Lord Albert was a clever man. He was careful with his food and wouldn't have eaten anything he knew had nuts in."

"Which means someone put them in his food," I said.

"Not me." Emma slammed three mugs on the table and gestured at the worn wooden seats set around it.

I settled into a seat next to Helen. "We're not saying you had anything to do with it, but you could help us figure out who's the most likely suspect. Who'd want to kill Lord Albert?"

Emma considered us both for several seconds before nodding. "I suppose there's no harm in that. But be careful asking all these questions. If Lady

Kate hears about this, you'll be the next two out the door. She doesn't like anyone poking into her private affairs."

"Do you think that's suspicious?" I said. "Could there be a reason she wants to hide the truth about what happened that night?"

Emma sucked in a breath, and her eyes widened. "You think she did it. What are you, a pair of undercover police officers?"

"No. Nothing like that," I said.

"We're just too curious for our own good." Helen grinned at Emma. "Some people call us nosy."

Emma passed around the mugs of tea and settled at the table opposite us. "I can't say I'm disappointed Lord Albert's death is still being looked into. The police focused on me during their investigation. They kept coming back to the fact I was in charge of the meals, and it was my responsibility to make sure those nuts weren't near the food. But how could I be responsible for something I didn't know about?"

"That doesn't sound fair. Did they question everyone else?" I said.

"They did. The whole family. I don't know what they were asked, but I was the one who kept getting grilled. I was certain they were going to slap the cuffs on me and send me away for good."

"But the police found nothing?"

"Of course not. That didn't stop Lady Kate from ruining my life. She fired me and bad-mouthed me to everyone. It was humiliating. I've only just started leaving the house again. I can't stand all the gossip."

"She must be as angry and confused as you," Helen said.

"I doubt that. She got everything after Lord Albert died. And I know she wants that house to herself. Well, her and her creepy son. Have you met Julian? The poor boy is unstable."

"In a way. I did almost hit him with my car," Helen said.

"Oh! Of course. Well, the household was always happy until Lady Kate got her feet under the table and Julian started skulking in the shadows."

"Julian sounds troubled," I said.

"He's even more troubled since Lord Albert died. Wretched boy." Emma drank down most of her tea. "I loved my job. All I wanted to do was serve that family to the best of my abilities. Lord Albert used to joke I was like an old piece of trusty furniture. Worn around the edges but always reliable."

"Lord Albert must have liked you."

Emma dabbed her eyes with a hanky. "I think he did. And I adore Celeste. She can be a little odd, though."

"Odd how?" Helen asked.

"She talks about seeing imaginary people. I'd find her at the bottom of the garden talking to thin air. She used to say she was talking to the fairies. I let it pass. After all, children have big imaginations. I have three boys, all grown, and they were the same. The strange thing about Celeste is she never grew out of it. She kept talking to her make-believe friends."

"That's unusual." Helen glanced at me and raised her eyebrows.

"Just before I was fired, she was talking to no one in the hallway. It gave me the chills though, because she kept saying Daddy, as if Lord Albert was there. It's no wonder the young woman has never had a boyfriend. You'd have to be a special guy to accept those eccentricities. Maybe it's something that runs in the family, since Julian is also touched in the head, if you get my meaning."

"Tell us more about Julian," I said. "We've not had a chance to meet him properly."

"I feel sorry for that young man. Mind you, with a mother like that, it's no surprise he turned out strange. He's always creeping around and insists on keeping his bedroom curtains closed. Occasionally, I'd force my way in and give the room an airing. The cleaning staff won't go near the room because they think he's so strange."

"Because he creeps them out?" Helen said.

"That and he's anti-social. But he's a young teenager going through an awkward growing phase. He's another one with a strange obsession. Not with fairies at the bottom of the garden, mind you."

"What's Julian's obsession?" I said.

"Ghosts. He's always talking to shadows. Usually, he'd run off if I got near enough to hear him, but I caught him a couple of times and asked him straight out what he was doing. That's what he said. He was talking to the dead. And a few times, I found him and Celeste talking to nothing together. Celeste joked about it and said she could see ghosts, too. She was humoring Julian, though. The boy has no friends. He's a complete loner. Tragic."

I glanced at Helen. Celeste and Julian both saw ghosts?

"What does Lady Kate think about his interest in ghosts?" I said.

"She's given up on him. She lets the boy run wild. That's why you almost hit him with your car. He's out of control."

"Do you consider Julian dangerous?"

Emma pursed her lips. "He could be, especially considering the way he's being raised. Lady Kate should be ashamed of herself. She's a terrible role model."

"I know you're still angry with her, but do you genuinely believe she had anything to do with what happened to Lord Albert?" I said.

Emma heaved out a sigh. "I wish I could point the finger in that direction, but she never went near the kitchen. She wasn't even interested in looking over the weekly menus I put together. She said that was my work, and I had full control. I don't think I even saw the woman make a cup of tea. She's always led a privileged life. Her father is the Duke of Bainbridge, so she grew up surrounded by serving staff and people doing everything for her. The idea of going into the kitchen and preparing a meal is alien to her."

"But Lady Kate has access to the kitchen?" I said. "If she wanted to, she could have intercepted Lord Albert's meal."

"I suppose so, but I was always in there, overseeing things. And we usually have at least one member of staff who serves on special evenings."

"Who served the night Lord Albert died?"

Emma tugged at her bottom lip. "No one. We were short staffed. There'd been a seasonal bug doing the rounds, and I was sending home anyone who even mentioned feeling unwell to avoid the family getting sick. I brought the food through already on the plates."

"Is that unusual?" Helen said.

"It happened once or twice a month. I'm trained in silver service waitressing, so I know not to make a mistake when looking after that side of things."

"Did the police check to see who went into the kitchen that night?" I said.

"I'm certain they did. And Lady Kate swanning around and getting in the way would have been noticed by someone. She was at the table the same time as everyone else."

That helped little with the investigation, other than to make it less likely Lady Kate was the killer.

"I appreciate your honesty," I said. "Given your history with Lady Kate, you could easily have accused her."

"I wish I could, but I'm an honest woman. I don't think she did it."

"If you had to pick someone, who would you focus on?" Helen said.

Emma sat back in her seat and inspected the inside of her mug. "I don't want to say. It doesn't feel right to accuse anybody."

"Anything we find out could be useful," I said.

"If I tell you, what will you do with the information?" Emma said.

"It all depends. If it's serious, we'll take it to the police. If it's just a hunch you have, we may look into it ourselves and see what we can find out." And talk to our ghostly friend to see what he knew, but Emma didn't need to know about the spooky side of this investigation.

Emma toyed with her mug. "If I had everyone in the household lined up in front of me, I'd point the finger at Lady Mary. I don't feel good saying that, because she's a sweet person, but she's struggled to move on. And it's unhealthy being stuck in that house. It's like she's trapped in her past and can't get free. She's been there all these years, so it must have affected her to see the man she married move on to another woman. And a much younger woman. That has to grate, no matter how kind-hearted you are."

"Has Mary ever mentioned to you she's unhappy?" I said.

"No! And you wouldn't know it to look at her. She's charming and kind to everyone. But it's not right, living with your ex-husband and his new wife."

"We have spoken to Mary," I said. "She admits her living situation is strange, but she stayed because of Celeste."

"That's one reason, and I've no doubt she's telling the truth about that. Celeste and Julian are sensitive children, and things affect them deeply. I remember when young Julian lost his rabbit. It was taken by a fox. He didn't speak for weeks, and I'd find him standing outside the empty rabbit hutch staring into it. They're very... I'm not sure how to describe it."

"Empathic?" Helen said. "I can be the same. I pick up on other people's emotions, and they impact me. If someone is feeling sad, I feel it, too."

"Perhaps that's it. I tried to comfort him and told him the rabbit had gone to a better place, but Julian shook his head and said that wasn't possible. He told me he hadn't seen the rabbit since it died. I tried to figure out what he meant, but he wouldn't explain it. He just said I wouldn't understand because I didn't see them. What was I supposed to think? Some little ghost bunny was hopping around, happy in its afterlife?"

It was entirely possible Julian had seen a ghost bunny or had been hoping to see it so he could have a goodbye with his furry friend.

"Going back to Mary, why would she give those nuts to her ex-husband?" I said.

"I never said she did. Don't put words into my mouth."

"Of course not. This is only theoretical."

"Hmmm. If you say so." Emma settled back in her seat. "I didn't get to see everything that went on between the family members, but I saw enough to know tensions were growing. Lady Kate was putting her foot down, and Lord Albert was getting older. I'm not saying he was senile, but you'll have noticed the age difference between Lady Kate and Lord Albert. I reckon Lady Kate was making her move to become the alpha, and Lady Mary didn't like it. I even overheard them arguing a time or two. Of course, the second they heard me about, they stopped. But there was friction."

"Friction that caused Mary to kill Lord Albert?" I said.

"She could have resented him for putting her in that situation. After all, Lord Albert divorced her, not the other way around. Even though Lady Mary always said it was for the best and she didn't love him anymore, I don't think she moved on. And she lives a sheltered life. She only goes into town once a month and has few friends. The poor old girl. She'll be next to kick the bucket."

Although I couldn't be certain, Mary and Emma must have been about the same age, so Mary was hardly decrepit. She seemed like she had plenty more good years in her.

"What do you mean, you think she'll be next?" Helen said.

"Lady Mary never got over the divorce. She'll die of a broken heart. She's only holding things together for Celeste. But something will push her over the edge. Maybe it already has. She had enough of taking a backseat and shoved things into action. She killed Lord Albert so she could be free. And with him gone, Celeste can leave with her."

These were serious accusations Emma was throwing out, but she'd had plenty of time to wonder about who killed Lord Albert. And she'd want to know who did it, since suspicion still lingered around her.

"Did you see Mary in the kitchen or anywhere near Lord Albert's meal just before he ate it?" I said.

Emma looked around, as if seeking inspiration. "I can't say I did. She came into the kitchen sometimes, though. She liked to make cakes. But she hadn't been in that day. And now I think about it, she took her meal to her room that evening. She wasn't feeling well. Lady Mary asked for something simple and then left."

"She wasn't at the table when Lord Albert reacted badly to the nuts?" I said.

"Well, no. But they could have been added at any time." Emma wriggled in her seat. "And just to be clear, not by me. I always had a soft spot for Lord Albert, and I'd do nothing to jeopardize my future at Drew House or his life."

I looked at Helen, and she tilted her head from side to side before nodding.

"Thanks for letting us talk this mystery through with you," I said. "We won't take up any more of your time."

"You're welcome. It's a comfort to talk about it to people who aren't trying to winkle a confession out of me. But you ladies be careful poking around. It can lead to trouble." Emma led us back to the front door.

"We will. But we want to make sure justice is done," I said.

"Maybe so. You'll end up losing your jobs, though."

"It's a risk we're willing to take. And wouldn't it be a Christmas treat to know what happened to Lord Albert?" Helen said.

Emma grimaced. "Not a treat, but it would. Keep an eye on Lady Kate, though. She's a sharp one."

"We will," I said.

"What's this?" Helen picked up a leaflet that had come through the door.

"There are carolers in the town today. The local churches come together and gather around the tree in the center. The singing is so beautiful. I was thinking of going, but I'm not in the mood." Emma tapped the leaflet. "You two should attend, though. Soak up the festivities while you're here. All the stores have displays in their windows, along with sale events for Christmas gifts. You'd enjoy it."

"Thanks. We might do that." Helen nudged me and nodded, suggesting we'd have no choice but to go. And I didn't mind a trip for some festive fun. It would be good to take a break from all the talk of murder.

We said our goodbyes and headed to the car. There was a light sprinkling of snow on the roof, but nothing to worry about.

"I couldn't find a reason for Emma wanting Lord Albert dead." Helen settled into the driver's seat, and I sat next to her.

"I agree. I could understand her killing Lady Kate, though, since she's ruined her reputation and now has no job, but Emma liked Lord Albert. I think we can rule her out."

"But something we're not ruling out is Christmas fun." Helen turned over the engine. "We deserve it. We've ruled Emma off the suspect list, so it's time for festive treats and carols. What do you say?"

"I say we need to keep digging into this murder." I lifted a hand as Helen began to protest. "But we can do that after we've enjoyed the Christmas indulgences."

# Chapter 7

"This is so beautiful." Helen's eyes glowed as we stood outside a busy tearoom in the center of the town. Overhead, twinkling fairy lights lit the street, giving it a warm, festive glow. People were bustling past, wrapped in thick coats and wearing hats as they carried their Christmas purchases.

The air was alive with laughter, and the scent of roasting chestnuts and warm spices filled the air. And to make things even better, Helen had made an amazing discovery.

She tugged on my elbow. "We have to try this festive cream tea. Cranberry-spiced scones with cinnamon-infused cream sounds heavenly. And look, they have an iced Father Christmas in the window. We have to try one of everything. This could be our only opportunity to have a magical cream tea. Lorna, please say yes."

I chuckled. "Why would I say no to all of that? I'm in."

We headed inside and had to wait a few minutes before we got a table because it was busy. Helen ordered two festive cream teas, and we settled in to enjoy a few minutes of people watching as customers came in and out to collect their orders, and servers dashed about with stacked trays full of delicious festive treats.

"I'm glad we saw that leaflet," Helen said. "I'd have never forgiven myself if I lost the opportunity to try cinnamon-infused cream."

A smiling waitress dashed over from the serving counter with a large, stacked stand containing four scones, a large pot of cream, three different sweet preserves, a plate of Christmas tree cookies with white and green icing, cinnamon swirls with a blob of cream in the middle, miniature pigs in blankets, and tiny filled pastries. There was also a large pot of spicy smelling herbal tea.

She set everything out with a flourish. "Enjoy. If you run out of anything, give me a shout. And the carols are starting in a minute. We'll open the door, so you can hear them."

"Thanks. This all looks wonderful." Helen was already swiping a thick blob of cream onto a scone.

I sampled a perfectly sweet and crunchy tree-shaped cookie. As I poured out the tea, I smiled as the first tuneful strains of Christmas music drifted through the café. The chatter inside faded as the customers listened to a rendition of "Silent Night".

"If we didn't have a murder to solve, this would be perfection," Helen whispered. "You have to try the cream. It's delicious."

I selected a scone, covered it in cream and preserves, and took a bite. My eyes fluttered closed, and I grinned as I munched on the tasty treat and listened to the sounds of Christmas.

Helen's finger jabbing my arm dislodged me from my peaceful musings. "Since we've discounted Emma, we should focus on Lady Kate and Julian."

"Agreed," I said. "Don't you think it's weird he's obsessed with ghosts?"

"You're a fine one to talk."

"What do you mean?"

"The ghosts. You spend most of your life around them."

"Not by choice. I try to ignore them. And if I remember rightly, you were the one who prodded me into helping them."

"You love being prodded into helping. And you'd help them even if I wasn't around."

She had a point. But seeing ghosts wasn't a hobby I'd encourage anyone to cultivate. I immersed myself back into the Christmas delights as the carol changed to "Away in a Manger".

Helen had just finished her second scone when her phone rang. She checked the caller. "I'd better answer this. It's Gunner again. The man is obsessed." Rather than taking the call at the table, she stood and went outside.

That was odd. Helen never hid her conversations with Gunner from me.

I pulled out my own phone and sent Gunner a message. *Are you free?*

*Yep. Nothing doing this end. How about you?*

I looked out the window. Helen was talking to someone, but it couldn't be Gunner. *Have you spoken to Helen recently?*

*Not in the last few hours. Why? She dropping hints about Christmas gifts again?*

*Something like that.*

*I forgot to tell Zach about your call earlier. I'm telling him now.*

*Thanks. It's nothing urgent. See you soon.* My appetite faded as I watched Helen laugh with whoever she was speaking to. What was she playing at? I trusted her, so I didn't think it was anything bad, but what if she was having problems with Gunner? Maybe she'd met someone else and was testing the water. I didn't want to think the worst of my best friend, but this was seriously strange.

After a few minutes, Helen came back and sat in her seat. "I'm having two cookies, then will see if I've got room for another scone. How about you?"

"I'm full."

"You can't be! At least have another cookie, so I don't look greedy eating on my own." Helen pushed a frosted cookie at me.

I took it and broke it in half. "How's Gunner?"

"The same. Looking forward to having time off over Christmas."

"We all are." I wasn't sure how to put my next question, so I decided on bluntness. "Is everything good between you two? Christmas can be stressful for couples."

Helen's eyebrows flashed up. "Of course. Great. Why wouldn't it be?"

"You're not tiring of married life?"

"No." Helen lowered what was left of her cookie. "Has Gunner said something to you?"

"No, nothing like that."

"He's said something to Zach, though? He's not happy with me?" She grabbed my hand. "Tell me."

"Relax. Nothing's been said to anyone about anything. I wanted to check in. You never know what goes on behind closed doors. Some couples seem happy, but when it's just the two of them, they're miserable. I'd hate to think anything like that was going on between you two. I want to make sure my best friend is as happy as she can be."

Helen tilted her head. "Lorna, we live together. We're behind the same closed door. You'd know if I was fighting with Gunner. You'd hear us yelling. We never fight quietly."

"I do hear you fight." My nose wrinkled. "And also when you make up."

She grinned. "There you go then. As frustrating as that man can be, I'm crazy about him. I've accepted I married a rough, tough alpha police officer. But that's okay, because he's also loving, generous, and funny. And he's the only man I've met who can make me snort laugh. We're good for each other. I introduce him to the finer things in life, and he shows me I don't have to spend a fortune to enjoy myself. And he's good with Milly. Any man who can look after a dog as well as he does is well on the way to being the perfect parent."

"Oh! You're thinking about children?"

"Only thinking. The sleepless nights and endless rounds of feeds worry me. Gunner's work will keep him away most of the time, so I'll be in charge. But I'm not getting any younger, so I suppose we should get a move on." She set about her third scone. "I'm assuming you and Zach have talked about children."

"Not really. I mean, we like children, but I'm more suited to being a favorite auntie."

"Well, you can be a fabulous auntie to the children I have with Gunner. You have nothing to worry about. We're happy."

I was glad to hear it, but it didn't explain why she was keeping her conversation a secret.

We finished our food and rolled out of the café to join the crowd outside to listen to the carols. The snow was coming down fiercely, so we didn't hang around for long. We picked up a few gifts from the outdoor market and dashed back to the car.

"Wait, a second. Isn't that Mary?" I tugged on Helen's coat sleeve.

"She must be out Christmas shopping, too," Helen said.

"Let's offer her a ride home. If the snow gets worse, she may have trouble getting back."

"Sure. But hurry! Even I'm having second thoughts about driving in these conditions."

We dashed to the jewelers Mary had gone into and looked through the window.

"Whoa! That's a lot of bling. And it looks like Mary's selling, not buying," Helen said.

She was right. Mary had brought out a large bulging velvet pouch and unfolded it for the man behind the counter to inspect.

"You don't think she's hard up for money and having to get rid of her jewels, do you?" I said.

"Maybe Lady Kate is withholding funds," Helen said. "It sounds like Mary got little from the will after Lord Albert died."

"She won't have to worry for a while. Not with all that money the jeweler's handing over."

"That's a serious wedge of cash." Helen whistled. "Christmas has come early for Mary. It's a shame she had to sell her pearls to enjoy it, though."

"It looks like it's not just ready cash she's getting." The jeweler picked up the phone, and although I couldn't hear what he was saying, Mary was nodding along.

"A money transfer, maybe?" Helen said. "That bundle of cash could be a down payment."

Mary turned and looked at me. I froze. It was too late to grab Helen and duck. Mary's face paled, and she turned back to the jeweler, her shoulders tight.

"What shall we do?" Helen said.

"We can't run. She's seen us."

"We can't stay and watch. Mary will think it's weird."

Before we decided what to do, the door opened, and Mary appeared. There was no sign of the money, and although her expression was strained, she was smiling. "What a surprise. What are you doing here?"

"We came to enjoy the Christmas festivities." I hoped my flaming cheeks would be put down to the cold and not my embarrassment at being caught snooping. "What about you?"

She looked over her shoulder and eased the door shut. "I was doing some buying and selling of my own. As you just witnessed."

"You sold your jewels?" Helen didn't look the tiniest bit bothered that we'd been caught. "You're changing your style or getting into minimalism?"

"Not quite," Mary said. "Oh, dear. This is embarrassing. How much did you see?"

"Everything," I said bluntly. "You handed over a lot of expensive gems. It's been a long time since I've seen such a collection."

"Yes, I suppose it was a big sale. I've been collecting those for a while. Saving up for a special event."

"Collecting? Those were your jewels, weren't they?" I said.

"Um..." Mary glanced around and leaned closer. "I have an explanation. But to make sense of this, you need to come with me."

# Chapter 8

"Is this a good idea?" Helen whispered to me as we walked back to the car with Mary.

"We need to find out what she's up to. Something's off. Mary didn't answer the question about whether what she was selling was hers."

"She's a sweet lady. She can't be doing any harm."

"We're about to find out if that's true."

We got to the car, and Mary was happy to sit in the back seat.

"Where are we going?" Helen said.

"You're in for a treat. And since you're animal lovers, this will be especially magical," Mary said.

I twisted in my seat to look at her. "What are you doing that involves animals?"

"You'll see. Head out of town and take the first right at the sign for Fur Valley."

Helen did as instructed, and we soon left behind the festive lights and carols and were heading into the countryside.

"What does this place have to do with the jewels you sold?" I said.

Mary hummed under her breath for a few seconds. "I'll come clean. You caught me doing something naughty."

"Those weren't your jewels, were they?"

"No. But I'm selling them for a good reason."

"Who do they belong to?"

She hummed some more and looked out the window. "Isn't this view stunning?"

"Mary, you said you'd come clean with us."

She thumped her hands in her lap. "Very well. They were Kate's gems."

"You've been stealing from Lady Kate?" Helen said.

"I hate that word. I think of myself as a modern day Robin Hood."

"You need to add more to that explanation," I said.

"Kate is cold, and she has a mean streak. She's also a Grinch, especially at this time of year. And she hates Christmas."

"The party she's planning suggests otherwise."

"Don't be fooled. It's for show. If Kate could get away with it, she'd cancel Christmas."

"What does this have to do with you stealing from her?" I said.

"Albert was always charitably minded. He had several local organizations he supported. As soon as he died, Kate cut off contact with them. Albert would have hated that. So I carried on with his good work. And I made sure Kate paid for it."

"You take her jewels, sell them, and give the money to charity?" I said.

"That's the size of it. And it's not out of revenge because Kate got my husband. I had no hatred for Albert. With Kate, it's different. And... if I was going to kill anyone, it would have been her." Mary raised a hand. "I get my thrills by taking some of the many necklaces, rings, and baubles she hordes like a sharp-eyed magpie."

"Don't the jewelers question you about where it's all coming from?"

"No. I've used the same place for years. They know me, so never question me."

"Doesn't Lady Kate notice her things are missing?" Helen said.

"She has dozens of boxes of sparkle, and she rarely wears any of it. It's wasteful. If I still had the money, I'd invest it back in the community. I never understand people who hoard wealth and never give back. I've always thought being a billionaire should be illegal. Who needs all that money? Anyway, where we're going will show you what I do with the money. It's a place where Christmas magic happens."

A few minutes later, we pulled up outside a beautiful old house with large chimney stacks at both ends and a sign announcing Fur Valley Animal Sanctuary.

I looked back at Mary, my eyes wide.

She nodded and smiled broadly at me. "This is where most of the money goes. They're holding a Christmas fundraiser this evening, and I was planning to drop by with my latest donation once I'd finished in town. I insist you join me. You must see what I'm doing is for the greater good. Every fur baby needs a safe place. Don't you agree?"

"It's still stealing," Helen muttered to me.

Although I rarely sided with a wrong-doer, Mary's logic made sense to me. It broke my heart to think of any fur babies without a home and a loving family. "Since we're here, we'll look around."

"You'll be spoiled for choice. They take mainly cats and dogs, but you'll find a few rabbits and other small fluffies around the back."

As I climbed out of the car, Christmas tunes floated out from inside the house. All the windows twinkled with fairy lights, and there was a huge, decorated Christmas tree outside a door covered in dozens of gold stars with writing on them.

When I looked at one of the stars, I saw it was a financial pledge to the charity, and the donor wished the animals a Happy Christmas.

"Let's fill in one of these." Helen already had a blank star in her hand.

I willingly joined in and found the donation box tucked around the side looking nicely full.

"Mary! I was wondering where you'd gotten to." A tall, broad woman with bright red cheeks and a huge smile on her face engulfed Mary in a hug.

Mary returned the hug, laughing as she did so. "As if I'd miss this wonderful event. I brought friends with me as well. Helen and Lorna, meet Isabel. She's the angel who runs this amazing place."

"Everyone is welcome, so long as they donate generously." Isabel stuck out a hand. "We've got dozens of fur babies inside desperate to meet you. Are you looking to adopt?"

I shook my head. "I'm already taken. So is Helen."

"Don't write me off. There's always room for a couple more fur babies." Helen's eyes were alight with excitement.

"Helen! You have a dog and a naughty lizard."

"A tiny dog and a mostly well-behaved lizard. Perhaps we could find a dog friendly cat to fit in with us."

"You'll find a pet for everyone here," Isabel said.

"Before I forget, I did a little fundraising while I was in town." Mary glanced our way and winked. "I'm hoping it'll help you meet your Christmas fundraising target so you can install the new heating."

Isabel opened the envelope and gasped before fanning her face. "Thank you so much. You're always incredibly generous."

"And I've got extra funds to transfer electronically when I get home. I didn't want to come here carrying only cash. You never know who you might meet." Mary's twinkling eyes flashed my way for a second.

Isabel hugged her again. "You gave us a donation only last month. With this money, all the animals will have a perfect Christmas. Now, come on, everyone, right this way. We had puppies arrive last week, and they need constant entertainment."

I happily followed Isabel into the building. It looked like a giant cracker had gone off inside, loaded with decorations. And the place was crowded, with people wandering around, chatting, enjoying the Christmas treats laid out on a table, and taking part in games to raise even more money for the charity.

There were several chilled out dogs wandering around, happily accepting pets, and even a few cats sitting up on the shelves, keeping a close eye on the situation.

"As much as I admire what Mary is doing," Helen whispered, "should we overlook her theft?"

I tilted my head. My heart was full to bursting as I absorbed the wonderful work at the animal sanctuary, so it was tough to be impartial. "We should take it easy on her. After all, she's taking a big risk to help these animals."

Helen gave a mock gasp. "Lorna Shadow, you're aiding and abetting a criminal."

"She's doing what Lord Albert would have wanted."

Helen giggled. "Don't worry, I won't report you. And after spending only a few minutes in here, I completely agree. This place deserves the money much more than Lady Kate needs more diamonds."

Mary walked over with a plate of mini chocolate Yule logs, which she handed around to us. "How much trouble am I in?"

Helen looked at me, and I nodded. "We won't say anything. This place does great work."

"I know I'm breaking the law, but I love animals. Kate's not keen on them, though. I've asked numerous times if I could adopt a dog, but she always says no. And Albert supported Kate's decision so as not to annoy her." Mary sighed and shook her head.

"Kate is beastly for not letting you have a pet. You should sneak one in," Helen said.

"She isn't a monster, but I get so lonely, and she doesn't care about that. Still, I keep the loneliness at bay by giving plenty to this sanctuary. It's been my salvation. And I know, if Albert was watching over me, he'd approve. He could never understand Kate's interest in buying so much jewelry. He even confided in me once that he thought it was wasteful." Mary popped a chocolate treat into her mouth.

When I returned to Drew House, I'd talk to Lord Albert and get his thoughts on Mary's light fingers.

I touched Mary's arm. "While we admire what you're doing, you must be careful. You could get in trouble."

"Oh, if I'm arrested, I'll accept it. I know I'm stealing, but any judge will see what an amazing reason I have to take what doesn't belong to me." She grinned and jigged along to the Christmas music. "Besides, I may not have much longer left. Why waste time worrying about what may be? Live in the moment."

Helen's expression grew worried. "You're not ill, are you?"

"No! But what happened to Albert was a wake-up call. No more hiding. I want to help these animals, so that's what I'm doing. Kate and her baubles be damned. Anyone for a spiced strawberry tart?"

"If the police find out, I'm sure you'll get off with a slapped wrist." Helen took a tart from Mary's plate.

Mary chuckled. "That's sweet of you, my dear, but I've donated over a hundred thousand to this charity. That will earn me more than a stern telling off. But I'm old enough and big enough to accept the punishment, should it come."

I tried to hide my shock at how much she must have stolen. Mary had been busy! My gaze went around the room, and my shock faded. These animals deserved it.

After finishing our food, we spent a while looking around and playing games before Mary guided us away from the bustle.

"Come with me. They have a quiet area where they house the animals ready for adoption. It's away from the noise, so they don't get stressed." She winked at Helen. "Maybe we can twist Lorna's arm and get you that extra fur baby."

Helen clapped her hands together in delight, and we followed Mary into a long, warm, low-lit corridor. There were glass pens on either side, housing dogs.

We spent a happy hour wandering around, looking at the dogs, giving them treats and belly rubs, and falling in love with each one.

"The animals look well cared for," I said.

"All thanks to Mary's light fingers," Helen said.

Mary chuckled, obviously overhearing. "I'm glad my fingers could be put to such good use."

"How did this place get started?" Helen cradled a scruffy ginger puppy, who wore an adorable Christmas sweater to keep him warm.

"This building used to be a private residence," Mary said. "The owner was animal mad, just like me. When he died, he didn't have heirs, so he passed the building to a small animal charity. It's been here ever since. They celebrated thirty years last year."

"Working here would be my dream," Helen said.

"You can't wear high heels while you clean out an animal pen," I said.

Helen pursed her lips. "Watch me."

We headed away from the animal pens before Helen put her name down to adopt half a dozen puppies and wandered outside to admire the decorations.

"It's such a beautiful old building," I said. "I'm glad it found a purpose and didn't get turned into apartments, like so many do."

"This place is another reason I don't want to leave the area," Mary said. "I've grown attached. But if Kate forces me out, I won't be able to stay anywhere local. Everything is so expensive around here. I'll miss this charity if I have to go."

I turned the corner and almost collided with a tall man in a smart suit, wearing a sparkling red waistcoat.

He stopped at the last second and backed away, raising his hands. "I'm so sorry. I was miles away."

"Christopher, is something wrong?" Mary said. "Why aren't you inside enjoying the Christmas party with everyone else?"

"Oh, Mary. I didn't see you there." He kissed her cheek. "I'm glad you could make it."

"Your frown suggests otherwise."

He huffed out a breath and looked at his phone. "It's not an end of the world tragedy, but I've had a last-minute cancellation for a wedding. I'd offer the slot to another couple, but there's no chance they'd be able to get everything in place so quickly. It's such a waste."

Mary patted his arm. "Nothing bad happened to the couple, I hope?"

Christopher leaned closer and raised his eyebrows. "The husband-to-be ran off with the much younger nanny. And I was so looking forward to a Christmas wedding to look after."

"This place makes a perfect wedding venue. And with all the decorations, it would have looked magnificent," Mary said.

"Tell me about it. I'd better go and see what I can salvage. If I can't find someone to take the spot, I'll just have to eat my weight in Christmas candy." Christopher marched off, muttering to himself.

"Poor Christopher. He does a beautiful wedding. And this place is popular with couples, especially the ones who love animals." Mary turned and smiled at us. "Follow me. There's plenty more to see."

"Lead us to the fur babies," Helen said.

Mary paused and took hold of our hands. "Thank you for understanding why I do this. I don't delight in stealing from Kate, but it made me angry when she cut off those charities that relied on Albert's benevolence. It's not as if she doesn't have plenty of money, but she's from a different generation and more focused on herself. Kate doesn't see the bigger picture. Albert and I were raised to understand we lived in a privileged position and should reach down and offer a helping hand. I refuse to stop that because my situation has changed."

Helen hugged Mary. "What you're doing is incredible. We can help the next time you make a jewelry grab."

I gently tugged her back, shaking my head. "Or we'll just keep quiet about what we know, so you don't get in any trouble."

Helen pouted. "Oh, I suppose so. But where's the fun in that?"

"Not getting arrested and losing the jobs we've only had for five minutes would be kind of fun," I said.

Mary laughed. "Thank you for the offer. I'm not looking for accomplices, but I would appreciate your discretion. Now, this way. Let's raise as much money as we can for these adorable animals."

Two hours later, my purse was empty, and my heart was full of Christmas cheer. A number of animals had been adopted, several almost by Helen, and we left the party smiling and laughing as we returned to the house.

Once we'd said goodbye to Mary and headed to our rooms, I wandered into Helen's bedroom to be greeted by Flipper and Milly.

"What a wonderful evening." Helen flopped onto her bed. "I can't stop thinking about all those puppies. I hope they get amazing homes."

"I'm sure they will. What do you think about Mary?"

"Totally innocent."

"You're biased."

"So are you. Or you should be. She's even more animal mad than you."

"I'll check in with Albert about the jewel theft and get his opinion, but I agree. Mary is innocent. She loved what Albert did for the charities. And she's risking jail by carrying on his work."

"We're definitely hiding her light fingers," Helen said. "So, what should we do next to figure out what happened to Lord Albert?"

"We move on to a different suspect."

# Chapter 9

I couldn't stop laughing along with Lord Albert as he roared with silent mirth and bent over double. I'd just told him what Mary was doing with Lady Kate's jewelry and asked what he thought. His reaction told me everything.

"I take it Lord Albert doesn't mind what Mary's been up to?" Helen was perched on the edge of her seat by my desk in the office.

"He thinks it's hilarious."

"What's hilarious?" Celeste skipped into the room. "What's going on with Daddy? I haven't seen him look that happy for a long time."

I wiped my eyes. "I told him some news he found funny."

"What's that? I need a laugh."

I looked at Lord Albert, and he nodded, gesturing for me to tell Celeste what we'd discovered about her mother last night.

I glanced at Helen, and she shrugged. "I don't see the harm. Celeste, can you keep a secret?"

"Of course! What's going on? I must know."

"This is serious. If you don't keep this between us, it'll get your mother in a lot of trouble," I said.

"I'd never want that. What is it?"

"We went to town yesterday and found your mom selling Lady Kate's jewels. She's donating the money to the Fur Valley Animal Sanctuary."

"Oh, that! I thought it was something bad. I often see her sneaking into Kate's room." Celeste looked at her dad. "Did you know about this?"

He shook his head and pointed at me.

"I have the cleverest mother in the world. I think it's genius. And Daddy loved Fur Valley. We used to go there once a month when I was younger. I haven't been for years, though."

"You see why we need to keep this a secret," I said. "What Mary is doing is illegal."

"I won't say a word." Celeste laughed along with her dad. "As you can see, we thoroughly approve."

Lord Albert nodded. He gestured at Celeste for her phone, then spent five minutes slowly typing out a message.

When I looked at it, it read: *Kate spends too much*.

Celeste also read the message. "He's right. I'd love to help steal stuff from Kate. I'll get involved with the next jewel heist."

"Maybe not. This is Mary's special project," I said.

"And she's good at it. Besides, your mother wouldn't want to risk you getting in trouble," Helen said.

"Oh, very well. I'll find something else to do. I'm glad you made Daddy laugh. He hasn't been happy, recently. You ladies are the perfect tonic for him."

"I expect he hasn't had much to chuckle about for a while." My laughter faded. It was time to get down to business. "And what I'm about to ask you won't make him happy."

"What's that?" Celeste said. "Do you have bad news?"

"In a way. Everyone in this house is a suspect in your dad's murder. That includes you."

"You need to find out my alibi?" Celeste bit her lip.

"To eliminate you from the investigation," I said.

Lord Albert's smile vanished. He frowned at me and shook his head.

I lifted a hand. "I know. But we have to question everyone. Celeste, what was your alibi for the night of your dad's death?"

"I was at the dinner table when he started choking. I'll never forget it. It was awful. He went bright red and swelled up. His lips, tongue, and his throat. It happened so quickly."

"Did you have access to the kitchen that night?" I said.

"Of course. We all do."

"And did you go in there?"

"No! And I can't cook to save my life. I also rarely eat nuts. I avoid all fat so I don't put on weight."

"Didn't you tell us Emma made you eat chocolate outside because it had nuts in it?" Helen said.

"That doesn't count. Dark chocolate is a health food. I read about that online. I don't much like nuts, anyway. I only ate that bar because of the yummy chocolate."

"Are you sure you didn't go into the kitchen that night?" I said.

She shook her head. "I never go in there. And when Cook was around, she knew when I liked my meals served and would bring them to me. I wouldn't have to ask. She knew when my stomach was grumbling. I stay away from the kitchen, so I don't get in the way."

"What was your relationship like with your dad?" Helen said.

"It was great. He was a sweetie. And for a long time, it was just me, him, and Mommy. I didn't even notice when things went wrong between them. It was a shock when the divorce was announced."

"Did you ever argue with your dad?" I asked.

"Nothing serious. We had little disagreements, but I was a daddy's girl. I never wanted to make him unhappy."

"What was your last disagreement about?"

"Nothing I can remember. Oh! I kept asking for a horse, and he didn't want to get me one. I already have four, but I'd seen a pretty mare with the longest eyelashes. He still said no. Mean old Daddy!"

That was hardly a reason to kill. "Will other people be able to confirm you were at the table when your dad had his allergic reaction?"

"Yes. I was with Kate, Julian, and Annie. And Cook was nearby, too. She brought in our food that night."

"Where do you usually sit at the table?"

"Always on the left side, near Daddy. Kate has the seat opposite me, and Julian sits near her. When he does sit. He's always moving around like he has itching powder in his underwear."

I tucked away that information. It meant Celeste would have had easy access to Lord Albert's plate.

"Did you see anyone go near his food just before he ate it?" I said.

"No, but I was secretly texting on my phone, so I wasn't paying attention. Phones aren't allowed at the table, but I wanted to buy tickets for a concert, and they were about to go on sale. I didn't want to miss the opportunity, so I was messaging a friend to see if she could buy them. I figured, between us, we'd succeed."

"Did you get the tickets?"

"I didn't, but she did. I was checking the screen when Daddy swelled up. I forgot all about the concert after that."

Lord Albert swirled in front of me and kept shaking his head.

"It's okay, Daddy. I don't mind answering these questions. And it's good they're doing it. It shows they're covering all possibilities. You should congratulate Lorna and Helen, not get angry." Celeste smiled at me. "You're good at this. Have you ever solved a murder before?"

I grinned at Helen. "We've gotten involved in a few mysteries." If only Celeste knew the truth about how often I saw ghosts and how many died in unfortunate circumstances.

"You can ask me any question you like. I want to make sure whoever hurt Daddy is found. I keep thinking it must have been Kate, but her lack of skills in the kitchen is making me wonder. She's worse than me, and that's saying something."

"If it wasn't Lady Kate, and it wasn't you or Emma, that leaves Julian," Helen said.

Celeste grimaced. "I never know what goes on in my half-brother's head, but I don't think he's a killer. He didn't hate Daddy, but they weren't close. Daddy tried with Julian when he was younger, but he's an insular person. He loves his own company and gets exhausted being around other people. That's why he spends so much time outside. He's a mystery to me. I always love meeting new people."

It looked like Julian was next on the list to approach. Although, how we were going to do that, I wasn't sure. I'd barely seen him since we'd arrived.

"Do you still think I'm the killer?" Celeste said, a tinkle of laughter in her voice. "Are you going to arrest me?"

"Um... no," I said.

"We hoped you might have useful information about who hurt your father," Helen said. "Of course, it wasn't you."

"Anything I can do to help. Now, Daddy, I need to text with you about my future living arrangements. And we have a horse to discuss. You must visit her. She's pretty, and she'll fit in at the stables."

His forehead wrinkled, but he nodded, his stern look still focused on me.

"We'll leave you to it," Celeste said. "Let me know if I can help in any way. The sooner this mystery is solved, the better." She left the room, grabbing her phone on the way out, and Lord Albert nodded at us before leaving.

"Celeste sounds as bad in the kitchen as Lady Kate. And Emma didn't mention seeing her in there.

I don't think she's involved." I looked over when Helen didn't respond. Her head was down, and she was texting. "Hey, is everything okay?"

"Oh, sorry." Helen kept texting.

"What's more important than solving this murder?"

"Oh, you know, Christmas things."

I arched an eyebrow. "Are you texting Gunner again?"

"Something like that." She sent her message.

"Helen, you would tell me if there was anything wrong between you two, wouldn't you? I know it might be tricky because Zach and Gunner are brothers, but I'll never tell Zach anything you don't want me to."

Her gaze shot to me. "We've already talked about this. Gunner is perfection. There's nothing wrong between us."

"You're sure? You can tell me anything."

"Positive." Her gaze shifted to her phone.

"Well then, less social media for you and more snowmen and mistletoe. We have a Winter Wonderland Gala to get on with."

***

"It needs to go up a couple of inches on the right." Helen stood by the tall stepladder I was perched on.

"I've already moved it up on the right. It can't go much higher." The house dressers had left, but I wasn't happy with the ice garland hanging over the front door. It was crooked, so I'd decided to fix it during our lunch break. It should have been a simple job, but unfortunately, I wasn't certain if Helen knew her left from right since we'd been trying to get the garland level for ten minutes.

"Hold it there," Helen said. "That looks right. Although... you could move it up a couple of inches on the left."

I sighed and grumbled under my breath as I stretched higher. The ladder wobbled, and I squeaked as I lost my balance. I was falling through the air, about to crash to the ground, when a strong pair of arms wrapped around me and softened the blow. I still hit the dirt, but with barely a thud.

When I looked up to see who my savior was, I discovered myself in Zach's arms. I stared up at him, not believing what I was seeing.

"Hey, beautiful."

"Hi! How are you here? What are you doing here?"

He grinned down at me, then kissed my cheek. "I heard you might be getting in trouble. And I'll always be around to save you if you ever need a helping hand."

My heart did a happy little hop at the sight of him, although I was just as thrilled not to have broken any bones falling off the ladder Helen was supposed to be holding.

"You two are adorable," she said.

Zach helped me to my feet, and I brushed myself down before looking at the ice garland. It hung forlornly at an angle, and I feared it was a lost cause.

"Well... You almost got it right," Helen said.

"Where were you?" I jabbed a finger at her. "You were supposed to look after the ladder so I didn't fall."

"I... I was checking my phone."

"I'll get Flipper to bury your phone in the backyard if you don't stop obsessing over it." I made a grab for it, but Helen danced out of my way.

"I never obsess. But I have to keep on top of my social media. And the work calendar is on here. Maybe I was checking that."

"I could have broken my ankle, like Annie. Or worse."

"Zach's here. He protected you. And he always will." Helen batted her lashes.

"You've got that right," Zach said.

I turned to him, still not happy with Helen. "It's great to see you, and thanks for the save, but what are you doing at Drew House?"

"I had a couple of jobs not far from here that needed quotes. Once I finished up, I figured I'd surprise you and see how you were getting on."

I grinned at him. "I didn't know you'd be working out this way. Are the jobs starting soon?"

"No, and they just wanted costings. I may not get them." He slung an arm around my shoulders. "Besides, you know how quiet it is this time of year for gardening jobs. I figured we could take time off, and you can show me around. It's a nice-looking house."

"It is. And I'd love to spend time with you. I need to work this afternoon, but I'm free in the evening."

"Then I'll stick around. I'll do some exploring and catch up with you once you're done with work."

"Lorna, Lady Kate was looking for you," Helen said.

"She was? When was this?" I turned away from Zach.

"When you were up the ladder. She didn't want to disturb you, in case, well, in case you fell. I'm sure she wants you, though. She was looking out the door and gesturing."

"Maybe she wants to talk to you."

"Nope. I've done everything I need to with the catering. It must be some important admin work that won't wait."

I looked at Zach. "Sorry. Duty calls. I won't be long. Get Helen to show you to the kitchen, and you can have some lunch."

"Perfect. I'll see you later." He kissed me again, then strolled away with Helen by his side.

I headed into the house and looked around, but couldn't find Lady Kate. I checked the downstairs rooms, including her private study, but she was nowhere to be seen.

I went back outside to find Helen and Zach, but they were also missing. I even checked the kitchen, but they weren't in there. So, I went back to the office and found Annie sitting at a desk.

"Hi. How are you feeling?" I said.

"My foot is throbbing, but if I stay in my room any longer, I'll go stir crazy. I thought I'd see if there's anything I can help with."

"I appreciate that. Have you seen Lady Kate? Helen said she needed me for something."

"Let me check her calendar." Annie clicked on a few buttons on her computer. "She's out this morning. She left early."

"Are you sure? Helen said she just saw her."

"Positive. And I heard the car leave. My bedroom is at the front of the house, so I often wake when I hear a vehicle outside. Helen must be mistaken."

Helen had definitely said she'd seen Lady Kate. Why would she lie about that?

"Is everything okay?" Annie said. "You look worried. I'm sure, if it's important, Lady Kate will find you when she gets back."

"Sure. And everything's great. It's just that people are being weird around here."

"I hope you don't include me in that statement. I mean, I say a few silly things when I'm on my pain relief medication, but I'm usually normal."

"No, not you." My gaze went to the door. I should find Helen and see what she's up to. Maybe she was joking with me.

"So... can I help with anything?" Annie said.

"Yes! I could do with a hand looking over the final list of attendees. You can fill me in about anyone I need to watch out for or anyone with special requirements."

"No problem. I've got a couple of hours before I need to take more pain medication, so I'm all yours."

I looked out the window but couldn't see Helen. She was up to something, and I didn't like it. But with a busy afternoon ahead of me, I couldn't worry. So I settled in at my desk and got to work on all things Christmas.

# Chapter 10

I'd been working with Annie for about an hour when she grimaced and shifted in her seat.

"Is your foot troubling you?" I said. "We could take a break, if you like. I always get achy if I sit for too long."

"Thanks. I can't stay comfortable in one position. Stupid ankle." Annie rolled her shoulders and rubbed her injured leg.

"It sounds like it was a bad break."

She nodded. "The worst. The doctor was worried about me for a while, and I really don't want to have surgery on my foot. The whole thing has messed up my Christmas plans."

"What were you planning to do?"

"Skiing in Aspen with my boyfriend. It's not something I'm great at, but I wanted to give it a go. Now, I'll be lucky if I ever get the chance to ski. This ankle will always be weak."

"Sorry to hear that. Hopefully, you'll get good news and won't need surgery."

"Here's hoping. I'm so grateful Lady Kate let me stay on and work. I don't want to lose my job because of this injury."

"How long have you worked here?" I set aside the file of seating plans I'd been browsing.

"Just over four years. Lord Albert hired me to be his personal secretary. Once I got his affairs in order, I worked for Lady Kate and occasionally Lady Mary, too. That keeps me busy, and it's interesting work. It could be anything from arranging international travel to hosting a private party at the house. There's also the less glamorous filing and admin, but I enjoy all of it."

"You sound like me. I love everything to have a place and be in order."

"Exactly! The family has always been good to me, the pay is great, and who'd complain about working in a beautiful place like this?"

"It's a perk of the job. Do you live here?"

"No. I rent a small apartment in the next town. But after I injured my foot, Lady Kate insisted I stay here. I've got my own room, and it means I'm able to keep working part-time while I recover."

"I'm glad you could stick around. Often, when I go to a new job, I struggle to figure things out. Everyone has their own way of doing things. Sometimes, their methods are a muddled mystery."

"I doubt you struggle with anything. You seem as organized as me."

"It's always good to have a plan." I smiled at her. "The family must appreciate you still being able to work for them, despite your injury."

"Honestly, I don't feel up to it, but I have to keep going. Jobs like this are in high demand. What if Lady Kate thinks I'm taking too long to recover?"

"I doubt that'll happen. After all, Lady Kate is looking after you. She wouldn't do that if she didn't want you to stay."

"Maybe she's feeling guilty." Annie pointed at her foot.

"Oh, I get it. Didn't you fall off a ladder while helping her?"

"I did. But it was my fault. I wasn't paying attention and stepped out when I shouldn't. Still, I'm worried she'll think I'm incompetent."

"You're competent. All the planning you've done for the Winter Wonderland Gala shows that. This is one of the easiest jobs I've ever had. If Lady Kate has any concerns, I'm happy to defend your corner. She'd struggle to find anyone as good as you."

"I'd appreciate that. Maybe I'm worrying about nothing. Lady Kate hasn't said she's unhappy, but she can sometimes be frosty, so I'm never sure what mood she'll be in."

"You're doing the best you can while dealing with a nasty injury."

"I am, but it's a struggle, and I want this boot and cast off. The doctor says it'll be at least another eight weeks. That's if surgery isn't needed. Then I'll have another cast, which doesn't bear thinking about."

"Perhaps your fiancé could help you if you need to take a longer break to recover." I nodded at the ring on her finger.

She twisted it around, a blush crossing her cheeks. "We're not technically engaged. He gave me this ring, and I wear it on this finger because I feel like we're official. We've been together a while, and he keeps telling me to stop worrying, and he'll make an honest woman of me soon. I'd just like to get settled."

"I'm sure it'll happen when the time is right."

She beamed at me. "Me, too. And although I'd love it if he could help me with my injury, he's away on business."

"He'll be back for Christmas, though, won't he? You won't be on your own, will you?"

"I'm not certain. I got the impression he was grumpy with me because I messed up our vacation plans."

I pursed my lips. "Are you sure you want this guy as your husband? My fiancé, Zach, wouldn't leave my side if I got injured." Something I did more often than I cared to remember, thanks to my ghostly encounters.

"I don't mind. His work is important. And I was the one who messed up by having an accident."

"He could be more supportive. You would be if he got injured. I'm certain of it."

Annie lifted one shoulder. "I've been promised a huge present, so that'll have to do until he's back home with me. Don't worry. I'm an independent woman, and I know how to take care of myself. The dashing boyfriend is a bonus."

"I get that. But sometimes, it's nice when someone takes care of you, especially if you've been in the wars." I studied Annie's expression, but she really didn't seem bothered about not having her boyfriend around over the holidays. "The family seems inclusive of staff. Maybe you could have Christmas lunch with them."

"They are. They're always good about inviting me to dinner and social events. It's different from other places I've worked. There's not all this upstairs/downstairs division. It has changed a bit since Lady Kate was widowed, though. I respect her, but she's not as personable as Lord Albert."

"Were you at dinner the night Lord Albert had his allergic reaction?" I said.

"I was. But it was only two days after I'd fallen off the ladder, and I was woozy from the medication. I didn't understand what was going on at first."

"It must have been a horrible thing to see."

"It was terrible. And I was powerless to do anything. I couldn't even get out of my seat because of this foot. The family was rushing around, trying to help. Lady Kate called for an ambulance, and Celeste rushed off to find Lord Albert's medication, but it was too little too late. Severe allergies are terrifying and affect a person so quickly." Annie let out a sigh. "Of course, I'd always known about Lord Albert's nut allergy. He mentioned it during my interview and said there was a ban on nuts in the house. I didn't object. If something is deadly to another person, you keep it out of their way. I still have the occasional nightmare about it."

"I expect you're not the only one."

"I even wondered about leaving after he died, but Lady Kate needed someone to deal with things. I even helped with the funeral arrangements. Lady Mary tried to assist, but that didn't end well. You may have noticed, the relationship between them is glacial. I do what I can to act as a go-between. It doesn't always work, but I like to think I help."

"I'm sure you do. And it sounds like you've decided to stay," I said.

"I have. Even though Lord Albert is gone, there's plenty for me to do. And you never know, Lady Kate isn't old, so she may re-marry. There'll be lots for me to do if the household grows."

Helen walked into the office with Zach beside her.

"Hey, you took a long time," I said.

"I've been showing Zach around," Helen said.

"Oh. I wanted to do that."

"Don't worry. I didn't show him everything. There's plenty more for you to do together," Helen said.

"Where did you go? I tried to find Lady Kate, but she'd gone out. Annie said she's been out all day. You couldn't have seen her earlier."

"She has? How strange. I'm sure I saw her in the doorway. My imagination is playing tricks on me." Helen's eyes sparkled. "Or maybe this place is haunted, and I saw a ghost."

Annie looked up from her desk. "Maybe you saw one of the cleaning staff."

"That'll be it," Helen said. "Problem solved without needing to invoke any Christmas spirits."

Annie stifled a yawn behind her hand. "I'm so sorry. I think I'll go for a rest. And I need to take my pain meds. If you'll excuse me."

"Of course. Thanks for the help today. It's good to have support when you need it." I shot a glare at Helen, which she ignored.

Annie grabbed her crutches and limped out of the office.

I gestured Helen to ease the door shut.

"Were you talking about Lord Albert?" Helen said.

I nodded. "Annie was there when he died, but she'd just broken her foot, so we can rule her out, since she could barely move. She still seems to be in a lot of pain from her injury."

"A bad break can mess you up for months," Zach said. "When I was a teenager, I got injured playing ice hockey. My leg was broken in three places, and I still wasn't right six months later. What happened to Annie?"

"She fell off a ladder in the library," Helen said.

"Nasty." Zach winced. "Helen's been getting me up to speed on what's going on. You've got a ghostly friend?"

"Yes, and all his family are suspects," I said. "Although I'm ruling out Mary."

"The ex-wife," Helen said helpfully.

"And I don't think it was Emma."

"She was the cook I was telling you about," Helen said.

"Who does that leave you with?" Zach said.

I leaned back in my seat. "Lady Kate, Lord Albert's second wife, and his son, Julian. And Celeste, his daughter."

"Celeste can also see her dad's ghost," Helen said.

Zach's eyebrows rose. "Interesting."

"So does Julian. Although he's odd and has terrible manners," Helen said.

"You will be careful looking into this murder, won't you?" Zach said to me. "I don't want you getting in trouble."

"When do I ever get in trouble?" I grinned at him.

"Just about every time you help a ghost. You should focus on mistletoe and mulled wine, not murder."

"I can't focus on the festivities until I've helped Lord Albert. It would be wrong to leave him in the cold, while everyone else is pulling crackers and overindulging on food. Someone in this family hurt him, and we need to find out who."

"You don't want a miserable ghost following us home," Helen said. "That's a surprise no one wants in their Christmas stocking."

I nodded. "Exactly. Solve the mystery, and the ghost will leave."

Zach narrowed his eyes. "A Christmas ghost is a surprise no one wants. Just be careful."

"How about you sneak off early this afternoon?" Helen said to me. "I'll cover things here, and you and Zach can spend time together."

"Well, since he came to see me in the first place, that would be nice." I was still annoyed with Helen for keeping secrets, and my words came out sharp.

Her eyes widened a fraction. "I've got things to check with the tree dressing outside, so you go have fun. It sounds like you need it. I don't want you turning into a Christmas scrooge."

Zach caught hold of my hand and squeezed it, stopping me from making a tart response. "Show me around the village. Then I'll take you for an early dinner."

My anger softened, and I smiled at him. It would be good to spend time together, and it would give me a chance to grill him over what was going on with Gunner and Helen. "Since Lady Kate is out, she won't notice I'm missing."

"And you didn't take a lunch break," Helen said. "If she comes back and asks where you are, I'll tell her you're on a work errand. She trusts us and has seen how hard we work. Lady Kate won't begrudge you a couple of hours off so you can spend time with your fiancé."

"Grab your coat and boots, and we can take Flipper for a long walk and then find somewhere quiet to eat. Jessie's in the Jeep, and she'd love to see him," Zach said.

"It's a date."

An hour of brisk walking through the Berkshire countryside with my favorite guy, his dog, and my best furry buddy cleared what was left of my gloomy mood. My cheeks were glowing and my ears tingling as Zach led me into a quaint little pub for food. He went and ordered for us at the bar, while I knocked snow off my boots and settled into a cozy chair by an open fire.

Flipper and Jessie curled up by the fire and instantly went to sleep.

Zach returned with a pint of ale for himself and a white wine spritzer for me. Neither of us spoke for several minutes as we enjoyed thawing out and sipping our drinks.

"The food will only be a few minutes," Zach said. "I ordered us the gammon and sweet potato pie with cranberry stuffing and roast vegetables."

"Sounds perfect. I need something hearty after that walk." Once I was warmed through, I shrugged off my jacket and placed it over the back of the chair to dry out.

"Despite the ghost problem, you're enjoying this job?"

"Yes. There have been no surprises so far. Not even from the ghost." I sipped my drink. "But I have been meaning to talk to you about something non-work related. Have you noticed anything strange going on between Gunner and Helen?"

"Can't say I have. But you know I'm not the most observant guy with relationships."

"You're observant enough. At least with me. Helen's been acting strangely. She keeps sending messages and receiving phone calls she doesn't want me to hear."

"You think they're from Gunner?"

"That's just it. They can't be. At least, not all of them. She's not been telling the truth all the time. Helen said she was talking to Gunner, but I was on the phone to him. Why lie about that?"

"That is odd," Zach said. "Are you sure Helen didn't make a mistake? She can be adorably ditzy."

"It's one reason I love her, but I doubt she'd make a mistake like that and tell me she was talking to a different person."

He scrubbed at the scruff on his chin. "I can't think what else it could be."

"Gunner's not said anything about them having problems?"

"Nothing like that. But you know what he's like. He'd rather talk about anything other than his feelings."

"I know someone else like that."

"So do I." He chinked his glass against mine. "Yet, somehow, I got you to agree to marry me."

"Did you ever have any doubt?"

"Some. You're a hard lady to pin down."

I grinned and leaned against him for a second.

"Do you remember how tricky it was to get Helen and Gunner together?" Zach said.

"Urgh! It was like pulling teeth from a rabid hippo. But I've always thought they worked well. They seem like a happy couple. Although..."

"What is it?"

"I wondered for a second if Helen's met someone else."

Zach lurched forward in his seat. "She's not cheating on Gunner!"

"I don't want to think that, but why is Helen keeping these secrets and pretending she's talking to him when she's on the phone with someone else?"

"I'm certain they're okay." Zach drank down some ale. "Gunner did mention he was stressed, though."

"About what?"

We paused the conversation as our food was brought over.

Zach sliced into his pie to allow the steam to come out. "Gunner's been talking to Helen about having a family. He'd like a lot of children."

"Kids? We were just talking about children. That must be it! Gunner's getting broody, and Helen's not ready. They're arguing over the number of babies to have and when to start a family."

Zach let out a sigh and nodded. "It's possible. And it could be what's causing tension between them. It's only a guess, though."

"But who is Helen speaking to in secret?"

His mouth twisted to the side. "I couldn't tell you."

"A counselor? Could things have gotten tense, so they need expert advice?"

"Maybe. Or we could have the wrong end of the stick, and it's got nothing to do with starting a family. It was just a thought." Zach shoved a huge potato in his mouth.

My food was forgotten as I thought through all the stumbling blocks they could be facing. "If Gunner wants a big family, they can't wait around too much longer. Or maybe Helen is speaking to a fertility doctor to make sure everything is working okay. Or—"

"Or you're getting ahead of yourself," Zach said. "I'm not even sure that is the reason. Maybe it's nothing. Helen could be getting her conversations muddled, and you're reading too much into it."

"This has to be it. I'm certain of it. I'm going to speak to Helen. We can help."

"With our extensive experience of having our own children, you mean?"

"Well, we have a fur family. That's almost the same thing."

Zach chuckled. "We do. And of course, whenever they need us, we'll help. But don't grill Helen too much. It's a sensitive topic."

"I won't grill her, but I'm her best friend. She could need me."

Zach tucked into his food, then turned the conversation away from Helen and Gunner. While I answered his questions about Christmas, in my head, I was laser focused on helping Helen. Tomorrow, I'd make sure she knew she had all the support she wanted. I was a natural fur mother, so I was sure baby advice wouldn't be that much different.

Just as we were finishing our meal, the bartender came over. "Sorry, folks, we're closing early tonight. I don't know if you've noticed, but the snow's coming down fast, and we don't want anyone getting stuck and unable to get home."

I'd been so engrossed in my thoughts about Helen and Gunner's new family that I hadn't noticed the snow.

"Thanks." Zach glanced out the window. "We should hurry. We don't want to get stuck outside in this."

"Definitely not. We need to move." We paid the bill, bundled into our thick coats, and headed out into the darkening evening with Flipper and Jessie. After a quick check on my phone, I discovered a shortcut to the house that would shave half an hour off the return journey.

Even though the snow pelted down and froze my nose, I was happy to trudge through the snow with Zach, Jessie, and Flipper by my side, talking about Christmas and all things holiday related. I tried hard not to dwell on Helen and Gunner, but it wasn't easy.

All too soon, we were back at Drew House and kissing goodnight.

I let out a contented sigh as I got inside. I still had my ghost's problem to solve, but at least I'd figured out what was going on with Helen. First thing tomorrow, I'd make sure she knew she could rely on me to make their baby plans perfect. Whatever she needed, I'd be there for her.

# Chapter 11

Although it had snowed most of last night, the brilliant morning sunshine had melted some of it away. The sky was a bright blue as Helen eased the SUV through the town and toward a truck full of gala supplies that had gotten stuck in a snow drift.

Helen flashed the SUV lights at the driver, who was perched on the front bumper, looking miserable. He raised a hand in acknowledgement and headed around the back of the truck.

Helen parked behind him, and we both hopped out.

"I'm glad you ladies could get to me," the driver said. "The roads are slippery. You think they'd get the gritting lorries out when it's as bad as this. But no! We're left to slide around like we're ice skating champions on wheels. I deserve a pay raise for doing this job."

"The gritting lorries don't always make it out to these remote spots." I hopped into the truck and pulled out the boxes from the back.

The driver grumbled under his breath as he watched me. "You can't see the ice on the roads.

That's where the trouble lies." He seemed happy to stand back and let me and Helen do the work.

"You need snow tires," Helen said.

"There's no point. We only get snow a few times a year around here. Waste of money."

"You're wasting your day, since you got stuck in the snow," Helen said.

"You know much about driving in hazardous conditions, do you?"

"Probably more than you do," Helen muttered to me. She beamed at the driver. "Oh, no. I just like the snow. It's so pretty. It makes everything sparkle. Maybe the sparkle distracted you."

The driver grunted in acknowledgement, his head turning as he peered along the road. "That's my tow arriving. You ladies need to hurry. You can't be on board when this thing is dragged out of the snow." He walked over to greet the tow truck driver, who was edging closer in a large red truck of his own.

"He's a charmer," Helen said. "I expect all the single ladies want to find him in their Christmas stocking this year."

I chuckled. "Let's get these boxes in the SUV and get out of here. My toes are already numb. I can't believe how cold it's gotten."

We unloaded the truck in twenty minutes, but rather than going back to the house, I pointed at a parking spot not far away. "Pull in here for a few minutes."

"Sure. Do you need something?" Helen expertly parked the SUV.

"There's a store I want to look around. You'll love it." I hopped out of the car, leaving Flipper behind to guard the boxes. I made sure the window was cracked open so he could get fresh air, but wouldn't be too cold.

"Is it a chocolate shop? Or a bakery? I can never resist a fresh pastry," Helen said.

"Neither of those. Right this way." I'd spotted 'Babies, Booties, and Bassinets' on our first visit to the town. I led Helen to the window display and looked at it. "What do you think?"

"This is cute. Look at the dolls dressed up as Christmas fairies."

"Let's go inside."

"Oh, if you're sure."

"Yep. Right this way." I headed to the door, Helen lagging behind me. The interior was painted a pale yellow, and there were rows of adorable tiny baby clothing, toys, cribs, and all the paraphernalia you needed for a newborn and beyond.

Helen stood beside me, taking it all in. "Wow! I didn't know you could get so much stuff for little ones. Do they need all these things?"

"I've no idea, but I thought it would give you a few ideas. Let's look around."

Helen wandered along behind me. "Ideas for what? I don't have to buy Christmas gifts for any children."

"Maybe you will need to soon."

"Oh, I get it. You and Zach are thinking of having kids? But I thought you were happy being an auntie?" Helen set down a cute pink teddy bear with a red bow tie.

"No, we're not planning for a new arrival, but I figured you and Gunner might be soon." I waggled my eyebrows at her.

Her nose wrinkled. That wasn't the reaction I was expecting. "Eventually, but we're in no hurry. I already told you that."

"Don't you want a big family, though? And you're both in your thirties. You don't want to hang around too much longer if you want loads of children."

"Whoa! Who's talking about loads of kids? Do you see this fabulous figure? A bundle of babies popping out would ruin it."

"You don't want a large family?"

"One or two. I mean, I figured we'd have one and see how we took to being parents." Helen shook her head. "But children are a huge responsibility. Plus, they're expensive. And I wouldn't be working full-time once I had kids, so we'd have to see how many we could afford. Gunner earns a decent wage, but he'd have to become Chief of Police to pay for lots of babies. And then there's the education fees, trust funds, so much to think about. No, we don't want a big family."

"Err... I guess I got it wrong."

"No kidding." She gave me the side eye. "I figured you brought me in here so you could look at baby stuff for yourself. You've been with Zach longer than I have Gunner. And you're older than me if we're comparing biological clocks."

"By a few months!"

"It all counts." Helen cocked her head. "Lorna, what's going on?"

I didn't want to admit I'd been gossiping about her with Zach. "Haven't you been talking to Gunner about having a family? I'm sure he mentioned something about wanting lots of children."

"He hasn't to me." Helen crossed her arms over her chest. "We're planning more long vacations and self-indulgent lie-ins at the weekend before we're grown up enough to have kids. It's bad enough with the pets demanding our attention. Wait! Has he said something to you?"

"Oh, no. I mean, maybe in passing, but I could have misheard. Look at this cute stuffed rabbit." This was going wrong. I'd expected Helen to come clean about the plan to start a family. Maybe she was worried it wouldn't work out or was scared something would go wrong, so she had kept things quiet.

Helen ignored the rabbit. "If Gunner wants an Olympic swim team of children, he needs to talk to me first. I'll be doing all the hard work by bringing them into this world."

"He's not making plans without you," I said hurriedly. "Forget I said anything."

"I can't forget!" She reached into her purse. "I should call him."

I caught hold of her arm. "I'm only trying to help. If you're attempting to start a family and things aren't going well, I'm here to support you. A shoulder to cry on, a cushion to hit, a friend to eat cake with. Whatever it takes."

Confusion crossed Helen's face. "I don't know where you've got this idea from, but we're not looking to have children soon. And I have no concerns about conceiving. It's something we want in the future, but not now. Really, you're being weird."

"Oh. I really thought…" I didn't know what to say, other than to admit I'd messed up.

"What did you think? Where did this come from?"

"From my overactive imagination. Sorry, I didn't mean to stress you out. I got the wrong end of the stick, that's all."

"You must have. One sprinkled in baby powder and smelling of overripe diapers. Are you sure I don't need to have words with Gunner?"

"I'm sure. Don't be cross with him if you do quiz him, though. This is all on me."

"Sure. I won't throw any accusations at him." She looked around the baby store. "Let's get out of here before my ovaries start ticking."

I was mortified as we left the store. How had I gotten things so wrong? Zach had planted the idea in my head, and I'd run with it. I was so desperate to figure out why Helen was being secretive, and it seemed so obvious when he mentioned the talk about children. But Helen's surprise was genuine. And her horror at the thought of having a huge family couldn't have been plainer.

But if she wasn't having secret phone calls about starting a family, then what was going on?

We'd just made it back to the SUV, when Helen shrieked.

I jumped and spun around to see her wiping snow out of her eyes.

"Someone hit me with a snowball." She looked around, trying to find the culprit.

"Duck!" I dodged out of the way as another snowball flew toward the SUV.

Helen grabbed a huge handful of snow and formed it into a ball. She flung it in the direction the last snowball had come from.

Several more flew toward us and whacked into the SUV, one skimming the top of my head.

"You keep the shooter distracted," I said. "I'll sneak around to see who it is."

"Don't worry. They won't know what's hit them once I've got my eye in." Helen was already forming several more snowballs, getting ready to launch.

I crouched as I skulked along a row of cars to remain concealed from the mysterious snowball thrower. They were hidden behind a hedgerow, but I could see movement between the branches. Several more snowballs flew toward Helen, and I heard her shriek again before a volley of snowballs slammed into the hedgerow.

I got to the edge of the hedge and poked my head around it. It was Julian. He was dressed in a thin-looking pair of black pants and had on a long-sleeved T-shirt. His hands were bright red, the same color as his cheeks, as he launched another snowball at Helen.

"Julian! What are you doing?"

He spun around and slid on the snow, landing on his back with a thud.

I hurried over to him. "Are you okay? Sorry, I didn't mean to scare you."

Julian remained in the snow, staring at me with large eyes. He opened his mouth several times as if he wanted to say something, but no words came out.

My shock turned to sympathy. "You must be freezing dressed like that. Let me help you up."

He slid out of my reach and shook his head. "I'm... I'm fine." The last word came out stammered.

"You don't look fine. Why were you pelting us with snow?"

His jaw wobbled. "I... I. Sorry."

"You wanted our attention? Do you need to speak to us about something?"

"It's you!" Helen peered over the hedge. "What are you doing throwing snowballs in my face? My mascara's smudged."

Julian's mouth flapped open and closed again, making him look like a beached halibut. The poor boy was frozen and now terrified as we loomed over him.

He gulped. "You... you still look pretty."

Helen blinked at him. "Oh! Well, thank you."

I deliberately took a step away. "I was going to suggest to Julian we get a hot drink."

The angry look on Helen's face faded as she took in the scene. "Of course. We need something to eat, too. I'm hungry after loading those boxes. Come on, Julian. You come with us. We're getting hot chocolate and sticky buns."

"Does that sound good?" I held my hand out to him. "Then you can tell us why you wanted to see us, if you want to."

He gulped again loudly before grabbing my hand and pulling himself to his feet. "Can we eat outside, though?"

"We're going into the café over there." Helen pointed behind her. "It's quiet, so we won't be disturbed. They have an open fire, so you can dry out while we chat."

Julian hesitated, looking around as if he was about to flee.

"You're safe with us," I said. "And I think there's something you want to talk to us about, isn't there?"

He nodded quickly. "I'll go in, so long as it's quiet. I hate loud noises."

"It looks almost empty. Come with us." I guided Julian around the bush.

Helen caught hold of his arm and tucked a hand through his elbow. "You make sure I don't slip. I always like to have a strong man by my side."

Julian's chest puffed out a fraction as he led Helen across the street and into the café. He hesitated by the doorway and looked back at me.

"In you go. I'll get our order, and you find a table with Helen. Pick one at the back, so we won't be disturbed."

Julian was shaking, but he nodded and headed off with Helen.

I grabbed our hot chocolate and some delicious-looking white-iced cherry buns and joined them at a table.

Helen had placed her coat around Julian's shoulders and was rubbing his chapped red hands between hers. "You hold on to that mug of hot chocolate to warm up even more." She pushed one over to him after I'd set the tray on the table.

He didn't object as he clasped the mug of hot chocolate and blew on the contents.

"So, what can we do for you?" I said after a minute of silence.

"I know about your ghost talent," he said so quietly I had to lean in to make sure I'd heard him correctly.

I glanced at Helen, and she lifted her shoulders. "That's right. I can see them." I checked around to see if anyone was listening, but we were the only people in the café.

"Celeste told me. You're not messing around? You really see dead people?"

"I do. I've heard that's something you can do, too."

Julian's gaze dropped to the mug. "Who told you?"

"That's not important. Is it true?"

"I don't like to talk about it. Whenever I say anything, people think I'm weird."

"I've experienced that, too. When I told Helen I could see ghosts, she thought I'd lost my mind."

"But then a ghost made himself known to me in a very inappropriate way," Helen said.

Julian stared at her. "What did it do?"

"He pinched my bottom. I jumped so high, I probably broke an Olympic record."

"He wasn't the nicest ghost I'd ever met, but it was a handy way to get the point across," I said.

"You believe in them now?" Julian said to Helen.

"Absolutely. They're real. And Lorna is great with them. She's been seeing them most of her life. She can answer any question you have."

Julian cleared his throat. "I've only been seeing them for about four years. When it first started, I thought I was crazy. They get intense and sometimes grabby. They scare me. I don't know what they want. I wish they'd leave me alone."

"I think that's often the problem. The ghosts don't know what they want, either. Some have unfinished business they need help with. That's usually where I come in, but some just drift around. They don't have a purpose. I think they're the ones that can be troublesome to the living. And you occasionally get poltergeists, too."

"They're the ones that throw things, aren't they?"

"Yes. They're usually not so nice to be near."

"Have you ever had to deal with a poltergeist?" Helen said.

"No. I keep away from ghosts, but it's like I'm a magnet. They keep finding me." Julian shuddered and sipped his hot chocolate.

"It scared me too when I first started seeing them," I said.

"But you've seen them all your life. You must be used to them. I keep hoping I'll get better or just stop seeing them."

"It gets easier. And I haven't seen them all my life. I had an accident when I was young and almost drowned. Since then, I've been able to see ghosts. There are some days, though, when I still get a fright if I'm not paying attention and something pops up."

"Not helping," Helen muttered. "Julian, most ghosts are charming. And the older ones can be interesting."

"Not the ones I meet," Julian said. "I... I almost drowned, too."

"You did?" I said. "What happened?"

"I was only a kid, and we were out on a yacht for a family vacation. Celeste pushed me into the sea. She said it was a joke, but I couldn't swim, and I've always been afraid of the water. She can be mean, sometimes."

This was surprising news. Whenever I'd met Celeste, she'd only ever been sweet. Was her good girl act a front to hide something more sinister?

"I'm sure she didn't mean it," Helen said. "Kids get carried away when they're playing."

"She meant it. I told her not to shove me, but she did, anyway."

"Do you ever talk to Celeste about seeing ghosts?" I said.

"Yeah. She makes out she's better than me because she's been able to sense them for longer, or so she reckons. She even told me I was faking seeing ghosts because I was jealous of her." He pulled Helen's coat around him. "If I could take it back, I would. I don't want things skulking out of the shadows and scaring me or pulling the covers off my bed in the middle of the night. A ghost even followed me into the bathroom. I almost jumped out of my skin when I accidentally walked through it."

"It is unsettling," I said. "Maybe Celeste didn't mean to say those things. You could have surprised her. And since you both see ghosts, it might be nice if you support each other."

"No way. I don't trust Celeste. She did this to me. It's her fault everyone thinks I'm a freak."

Helen bit her lip, her gaze full of sympathy.

"Do you see your dad's ghost?" I said.

"I do. He's not as scary as the others."

"Can you communicate with him?"

"I don't want to. I never liked the guy when he was alive. Now he's a ghost, he creeps me out."

"What didn't you like about Lord Albert?" Helen said.

"He didn't get me. He was the first one to suggest I go into therapy. If it wasn't for my mom, he'd have sent me to boarding school. I wish his ghost would get lost."

Julian didn't seem bothered about Lord Albert being dead. Maybe there was more to the story than he was letting on. Did he actively dislike his father when he was alive? "Were you there when your dad had his allergic reaction the night he died?"

"I came in at the end, but I was outside most of the time. Dad liked us to eat together, but I hate the dining room. There's a ghost that hovers around while you're eating. Have you seen her? She's ancient."

"I've not seen her," I said. "Does she bother you?"

"Of course. It's a dead thing floating in the air."

"Most ghosts don't mean you any harm. You should talk to this ghost and see if you can help her. If you can, she may leave for good."

He shook his head. "I don't want to do that. What if more chase after me and insist I help? That would be a nightmare."

"It's not so bad. You could communicate with your dad and help him figure out what happened to him. Not everyone thinks his death was an accident."

"It was probably Celeste who gave him those nuts," Julian muttered.

My eyebrows flashed up. "What makes you say that?"

"She had a huge fight with Dad. She hit him. Celeste has a wicked bad temper."

"What were they fighting about?" Helen said.

"I don't know. I heard the yelling, and then Dad yelped like he'd been injured. They have the same hot temper. They get angry easily, but then it blows out a minute later. I was outside, looking in through the window, when I saw them. Celeste really whacked Dad."

Helen shot me a meaningful look.

I nodded at her. This was an important detail Celeste hadn't mentioned when we'd asked about her arguing with Lord Albert.

Julian lifted his gaze to meet mine. "You don't think I'm lying about the ghosts?"

"Not for a second. If you want to talk about them, you know where to find me."

His shoulders sagged as if a weight had been lifted off them.

Helen nudged me. "It's snowing again. We need to get the gala supplies back to the house. Would you like a lift back, Julian? There's enough room in the SUV."

Julian jumped up and shrugged off Helen's coat. "I hate small spaces. If I'm trapped somewhere, it makes it easier for the ghosts to get me." He raced out of the café without looking back.

I stared after him for several seconds. "Julian is a troubled young man."

"You need to mentor him before he loses his mind," Helen said as she polished off her bun. "I'm no expert, but he needs help. He's terrified of ghosts."

"He does. It's sad. We both know some ghosts can be mean, but generally, they're simply confused. Help them out, and they're happy."

"Did you pick up on Julian's lack of love for his dad?" Helen said.

"I did. Although he said he wasn't in the dining room when Lord Albert ate those nuts."

"Should we keep him on the suspect list?"

"For now. At the moment, I'm more interested in Celeste. She's been hiding things from us." I finished my last bite of bun. "We should get back to the house and find out why."

# Chapter 12

Celeste hadn't been around yesterday afternoon when we'd returned from town. We'd unloaded the supplies, finished work for the day, and had dinner without the family.

I looked out the window, a smile on my face as I surveyed the beautiful, pristine snow in the front yard. My gaze shifted to a delivery truck inching along the gravel. It pulled up outside, and the driver hopped out.

Helen tilted her head as she noticed the truck. "Who's that?"

"No idea. I'll go take a look." I walked to the front door with Flipper and opened it.

The driver looked over and nodded. "Morning. I've got your trees. It took me ages to find this place."

"Trees? What trees?" I set down my mug of coffee and stepped into the crisp morning air. Flipper trotted out to do his morning business after giving the driver a sniff to make sure he was friendly.

The driver checked his clipboard. "Your three premium festive fir trees with dusted glitter. Where do you want them? They can be inside or out. It's up to you." He eyed the entrance, most likely hoping I wouldn't insist he lug them indoors.

I had no idea we were getting more trees for the house. There were three inside, and a large one outside Helen was in charge of decorating. "I'm not sure. You've definitely got the right place?"

The driver walked over and handed me the order form. Sure enough, there was an order for three eight-foot Christmas trees.

"They're here!" Celeste dashed past me in a fluffy pink robe. She clapped her hands together as the delivery driver dragged out the first tree.

"Did you order these?" I said.

Celeste nodded. "I wanted a fun, festive project. We always have professionals in to decorate, but that's boring. So, I figured, what's the harm in having a few extra trees?" She walked around the trees, stroking them through their protective netting.

"Where are you going to put them?" We stepped out of the way as the delivery driver heaved the trees to the front door.

"We could have one in your office," Celeste said, "and one in the kitchen."

"They're huge. We don't want them getting in people's way."

She shrugged. "I'll find somewhere. I'll have them all in my bedroom if I must."

"Where do you want the one in the pot?" the driver said.

"By the front door. It'll look pretty covered in twinkling solar lights."

The driver used a mechanical lifter to bring down an enormous fir tree in a ceramic pot. He set it on the driveway, then stepped back. "That's your lot."

Celeste scribbled her signature on the bottom of the order and handed it back before the driver left.

"I've been sneakily buying decorations, too." Celeste's voice was a conspiratorial whisper. "Kate always wants things done just so, but I like different colors on the trees, and I don't care if everything matches. I even got baubles in the shape of snowmen. Can you give me a hand to get them out of storage? I had to hide them, because Kate would disapprove and make me send everything back."

"Sure. But what will you do when Lady Kate finds out?"

"By the time she gets back this afternoon, it'll be too late. Once I've decorated the trees, she can't tell me to get rid of them. This way."

I grabbed a jacket, then followed Celeste around the side of the house to the barns, with Flipper by my side. "I met Julian in town, yesterday."

She gave an exaggerated eye roll. "I hope he wasn't causing problems. He's a nuisance."

"He was throwing snowballs at us."

Her head whipped my way. "Julian's an idiot. I hope you told him off." She pushed open the barn door.

"I'm worried about him. He seemed anxious."

"Anxious is his default position. He's got more so-called problems than I can keep track of. Most of them he makes up to get attention."

"You don't get along?"

"He's my annoying younger half-brother. Of course, we don't."

"But you would look after him, if he needed you to, right?"

Celeste was opening boxes and peering inside them. "Sure. Where did I put those decorations? I was certain I left them right here, but I can't find them. I hope no one has been snooping around."

"Julian told me he sees ghosts. I didn't realize that talent ran in the family."

"It doesn't. He's making it up. He may sense something vague, but he can't see ghosts like I can. I'm special." Celeste yanked out some green tinsel. "Got it!"

"Julian was certain about what he could see. And he's not happy. He'd appreciate some big sister advice on how to deal with the ghosts."

"I'd be wasting my breath. He never listens to me. Besides, I don't want to hang around with him any more than necessary. It's not fun to have your baby brother lurking about and complaining."

Flipper turned his head to the door and whined.

Celeste looked up and waved over my shoulder. "Hello, Daddy. You can stay, so long as you don't give away my secret Christmas mission. Not that you can, since you can't talk to anyone. This is just between us, got it?"

Lord Albert drifted over, a curious look on his face.

"We're hunting for decorations," I said to him. "Celeste ordered a few extra trees this Christmas."

His smile was indulgent as he watched his daughter hunting through boxes.

"Since you're both here, I have something to ask you," I said.

Celeste didn't look up from her continued search. "What's that?"

"I learned you argued with your dad not long before he died. And it got so heated that you hit him."

Celeste froze, her hands clenched around a box. "Who's been telling lies?"

Lord Albert zoomed to her side and tried to comfort her by patting her arm, but it only made Celeste shudder.

"Are you saying you've never hit your dad?" I said.

"I... I don't remember. Help me with these decorations. This is important. There are another four boxes we have to find."

Lord Albert remained close to her, his expression revealing his anxiety as his gaze flicked from me to Celeste.

"Celeste, a fight with your dad just before he died is also important. What was it about?"

She dropped the box she held. "I didn't mean for it to happen. I loved him. I still do." Her gaze went to her dad. "He wouldn't give me what I wanted."

"What was that?" I said.

"My independence. Living in the countryside is boring. There's nothing to do unless you like hiking through the woods and getting covered in mud. For Julian, this is the perfect place. He gets to run wild and see no one. But I want a life. I want to make friends and go dancing every night if I choose. And it's a hassle getting anywhere. I don't even have a car, so I have to ask permission to leave. It's like being in a prison."

"A luxurious prison, surrounded by people who care about you," I said.

"You're no help! I only want a small apartment, just for me. Four or five bedrooms in a pretty part of the country would be ideal. Or maybe abroad. I'm flexible. But Daddy wouldn't listen to me. He kept saying I had more growing up to do and needed to take on some responsibility around the house to show I could look after myself. But I'd have hired staff to deal with the tedious house business. He kept saying no, and I kept getting angrier. Suddenly, I hit him. I... I made his nose bleed."

Lord Albert tried to pat her arm again. He looked at me and shook his head.

A tear trickled down Celeste's cheek. "I hate myself for hitting him. The second I did, I regretted it."

Lord Albert nodded several times and shook his arms at me in a jazz-hands style, as if warning me to back off and leave Celeste alone.

"Was that the only time you hit him?" I said.

Her gaze narrowed as she looked at me. "What are you suggesting?"

"That you haven't been honest. You had a problem with your dad. He wasn't giving you what you wanted, so..."

"So I put nuts in his food to kill him?" Celeste strode past me to the door. "I thought you were my friend."

"Wait! You concealed your fight. Why do that?" I chased after her.

"I don't like you anymore." Celeste raced out the door.

Lord Albert zoomed after her, and I was quickly on Celeste's heels, Flipper dashing along with me.

"If you want me to find out what happened to your dad, I need to know everything," I said.

Celeste kept running, and Lord Albert kept up with her. "Go away! I don't want to talk to you."

"Flipper, get ahead and slow Celeste down."

Flipper barked, then raced ahead of me, quickly overtaking Celeste. He blocked her path and bared his teeth.

Celeste squeaked, skidded to a halt, and changed direction.

Flipper was off after her again.

"Call off your dog, Lorna. I thought he was nice, too. You've both deceived me."

"We're nice. But you need to talk to me. Tell me what's going on."

"I don't have to talk to you if I don't want to. You're not the police. If you keep chasing me, I'll make Mommy fire you. I'll say you scared me and set your horrible dog on me."

Flipper was still on Celeste's heels, but he hadn't touched her.

"Be reasonable." I looked at Lord Albert, who was keeping up with his daughter. "Can you help?"

He shook his head.

Flipper blocked Celeste's way again. She staggered back and hit a giant, glowing reindeer display set against one corner of the house.

The largest reindeer swayed on its huge legs before toppling to the ground. One antler cracked off, and the head rolled away.

"Now look what you've made me do." Celeste stamped her foot. "I love these reindeer. Now, one of them has been beheaded." She scooped up a handful of snow and threw it at me.

"What's going on out here?" Annie hobbled out the front door on her crutches. "I heard shouting."

I grabbed the damaged reindeer's head. "There's been an accident."

Celeste glared at me, a ball of snow in her hand.

"Oh, the poor reindeer." Annie looked at the carnage, her gaze flicking between us. "How did it get damaged?"

"I... I stumbled," Celeste said, some of her fire fading. "You know how clumsy I can be."

Annie hobbled nearer. "Don't worry. Lady Kate's out this morning, so we have time to clear up. And accidents happen."

"This is some accident." I stared at the headless, six-foot glowing reindeer. "How will we conceal this?"

Annie's gaze drifted over the mess before she nodded. "I'll say I whacked it with my crutch. Lady Kate knows how unsteady I am on my feet. She'll think I was the clumsy one. How does that sound, Celeste? No one needs to know you were involved."

"That's not so bad, I suppose." Celeste shot me another glare before dashing off.

Lord Albert looked like he was going to follow her, but then stopped and returned to me, shaking his head, disappointment and worry etched on his ghostly features.

I discreetly placed my phone on the window ledge, in case he had anything to say.

Annie let out a sigh. "What a mess."

"It is. I didn't expect to start the morning dealing with a decapitated reindeer." And Celeste had revealed her temper to me. Maybe she'd lost control after her fight with Lord Albert and gotten revenge by spiking his food. Would she be that spiteful? She struck me as more childish than malevolent, but children could be cruel.

"Celeste can be a handful," Annie said softly. "She's a sweet young woman but has been overindulged. She was the only child for a long time. I don't think that did her any favors."

"I definitely saw another side to her this morning."

"Celeste is... complicated. And she's prone to fantasies. I've seen her talking to imaginary friends. I always thought people grew out of that, but Celeste's never let go of those imaginings."

"I've noticed that, too," I said.

"You'll also have noticed, if she doesn't get her own way, she gets hotheaded." Annie lifted a crutch and pointed it at the damaged reindeer. "Did she deliberately knock this over?"

"She wasn't in a good mood when it happened, but she didn't do it on purpose."

Annie looked around, chewing on her bottom lip. "Be careful around Celeste. I don't like to gossip, but she almost got arrested for assault."

"Who did she assault?" I said. "Was it someone in the family?"

"No, no one here. But she was out for an evening with friends and got into an argument with another girl. It got vicious. If it hadn't been for her family's influence, she'd have gotten a criminal record. Lord Albert was friends with the Police Commissioner. He twisted a few arms, and Celeste got off with a caution. I heard she broke the other girl's nose."

The phone I'd placed on the windowsill lit up with a message: *stop her*. Lord Albert must be talking about Celeste, or maybe he didn't want Annie gossiping about his daughter.

"Have you ever been concerned about your safety around Celeste?" I said.

"Oh! No, nothing like that. And generally, we get along fine. But I must admit, I keep out of her way if she's having a tantrum."

My phone buzzed again. The message read: *lies*.

Annie glanced at the phone. "Is something wrong with that? The screen keeps flashing on and off."

"I've been having problems with a messaging app. I need to reinstall it."

"Well, it's almost Christmas. You could put a new phone on your Christmas list. You never know what Santa may bring you."

I grabbed the phone so Lord Albert couldn't keep messing with it and tucked it in my pocket. "That's a great idea."

Annie shivered. "I need to get back inside before I turn into a snowman. Oh, I meant to ask you about the extra trees I found. Did you order them?"

"No, they were Celeste's idea. She wanted to do some decorating of her own."

"That girl. When you overindulge children too much, they can turn into brats."

"I think she's excited about making Christmas special, especially after what happened to Lord Albert."

Annie's cheeks flushed. "Of course. Sorry. That was thoughtless of me to say. She must miss him. And Lord Albert was such a fan of this holiday."

I looked at the broken reindeer. "He wouldn't have liked seeing this destroyed."

"No, but he'd have let Celeste get away with it. I can't help with the clean-up, but one of the cleaning staff will be out soon. All evidence of reindeer foul play will be gone before Lady Kate gets back. And if she notices it missing, I'll hold up my crutch and admit responsibility."

"That's good of you," I said.

"I think Lady Kate feels guilty about my accident, so hopefully, I can get away with it," Annie said. "I was planning to work in the office for a couple of hours, so if there's anything you want to go over with me, just let me know."

"Great. I'll come inside in a few minutes once I've figured out where to hide this reindeer."

"I'll see you in there." Annie hobbled away.

I set down the damaged reindeer's head and stared at the house. My confrontation with Celeste was taking me in a new direction. I needed a plan of action to keep on top of my ghost, the suspects, and the upcoming Christmas party, or this festive season would get out of control.

# Chapter 13

I'd been waiting by the front door for five minutes before Helen rushed down the stairs. She was bundled up in a thick winter coat, scarf, hat, and gloves. Milly was tucked inside her coat, her little tufted ears just visible.

"What took you so long? Celeste just went out. If we don't hurry, we'll lose them." I marched to the front door with Flipper and peered out the window. I could still see Celeste and Julian hurrying away in the frosty gloom.

"Sorry. I couldn't find my hat. And I'm not going outside when it's this cold without covering my head. My ears always freeze and go bright red. Then they sting when they warm up." Helen's phone buzzed as we stepped out the door.

"Is that Gunner?" I said.

She checked the message and shook her head. "That's another reason I was late. I kept calling him, but he's not picking up."

After my run-in with Celeste this morning, we'd decided to do background research on her. That was where Gunner came in handy. He could discreetly check records of the suspects we were looking into. Just like Zach, he wasn't a fan of us investigating murder suspects, but he understood when there was a ghost needing help, we had to make things right. And if that meant a little snooping into their criminal records, then that was what he did for us.

"Did you find out where Celeste and Julian are going?" Helen walked beside me, her gaze glued to her phone. Flipper was on my other side.

My attention was on the yellow-tinged snow clouds overhead as we hurried along the driveway. "No, I just heard Celeste say to Julian to meet her at five o'clock."

"They could be going Christmas shopping."

"From what Celeste said to me, she doesn't like her brother much. Would she spend time with him if she didn't have to?"

Helen's phone buzzed. "At last! It's Gunner. Hey, what have you found out about Celeste?" She put her phone on speaker so I could hear the conversation.

"There's not much to tell. She does have a record, but it's minor stuff. The kind of thing entitled rich kids get in trouble for."

"Is there any mention of an assault charge?" I said. "I found out Celeste got in a fight with another girl."

"There's a caution on her record," Gunner said. "It details a fight she got into a year ago. From the information I discovered, she should have been charged. The other girl was a mess."

"See what you can get away with when you have friends in high places?" Helen said.

"Her dad knew the local Police Commissioner," I said. "Strings were pulled to hush up the fight."

"Ah, that makes sense," Gunner said. "It took me a while to dig out this record. I imagine it was buried by someone up top."

"What else has Celeste got on her record?" I said.

"Celeste was caught shoplifting when she was fifteen."

"Why would she need to steal?" Helen said. "She could have asked her parents for anything."

"Probably to get attention. It was cosmetics. Celeste got caught by a security guard, and her parents paid for the things she took. She was banned from the store, though. She was also caught with some friends, underage drinking. The group got a bit mouthy with the police who found them."

"From what we're learning about Celeste, she's got a temper," I said. "And she assaulted her dad not long before he was killed."

"I'm guessing that nugget of information was kept within the family after he died," Gunner said.

"It was. Lord Albert is adamant Celeste didn't mean to hit him. She was tearful about it, but then her temper flared."

"Celeste seemed so nice when we first met, but she's been hiding this from us. It makes me wonder what else she's been covering up," Helen said.

"You think she killed the old man?" Gunner said.

I nodded. "She's gone to the top of the suspect list."

"We're tailing her," Helen said. "Celeste and her brother, Julian. I told you about him."

"Be careful. Don't get yourselves in trouble," Gunner said.

"We won't, but we want to see what Celeste's doing. Her behavior is erratic, and her brother's vulnerable," I said.

"Are you sure you two aren't getting in over your heads?"

"We'll be fine. We have Flipper and Milly to protect us," Helen said.

Gunner sighed. "Milly can't fight her way out of a paper bag."

The little dog whined as if she knew she was being criticized.

"At least you have Flipper there," he continued. "He doesn't mess around when there's trouble."

"He'll look out for us." I petted Flipper's head.

"Good. Because I'd quite like to have my wife around at Christmas. Her best friend, too."

"You know us." Helen winked at me. "We never get into any difficulties."

Gunner's chuckle wasn't full of mirth. "I'll send Zach back to see you if you don't behave."

"Don't worry about us. Now, have you wrapped all the Christmas presents yet?" Helen said.

"Angel, Christmas is ages away."

"It's the middle of December. I don't want to find my Christmas presents still in their carrier bags."

"Would I do that to you?"

"Do I need to remind you about the birthday present I got that you'd wrapped in a hand towel?"

This time, his laughter was genuine. "I couldn't help the terrible wrapping. I'd been working three days straight on a fraud case. I could barely see straight, let alone figure out what kind of wrapping paper you might like. You're lucky you got a present."

"Lucky! You bought it from the garage on your way home," Helen said. "It was a car cleaning kit."

"At least you have a car to clean. It could have been worse," I said.

"How do you work that out?"

"Gunner remembered your birthday."

"They say it's the thought that counts," Gunner said. "And I made it up to you by taking you away for two weeks. You didn't have to lift a finger."

"That helped make up for the terrible gift," Helen said. "Anyway, we've got to go. We've got suspects to tail. Wish us luck. Love you."

"Hey, don't—"

Helen ended the call before Gunner could caution us again to be careful.

"I've not been out this way before," I said. The path we walked along was small and overgrown, so we had to go single file to avoid the spiky bare branches poking out from the high hedgerow.

"They're heading in the direction of the village. Let's get closer so we can hear what they're talking about."

"Be careful. We don't want them to spot us. Julian's so jumpy. If he sees us following him, he'll run away and never talk to us again."

We hurried nearer until their voices were clearer.

"You need to be more careful," Celeste said, her tone sharp.

"I am careful."

"You've been talking about ghosts to people you shouldn't. You'll get locked away. People will think you're crazy. Again."

"That's not nice," Helen muttered.

"I've only been talking to Lorna and Helen. They want to help me. They bought me cake and hot chocolate. And... Helen is pretty."

Celeste snorted a laugh. "You're a child. And you must have seen the wedding ring on her finger. Helen wouldn't look twice at you. Stop showing off in front of her by lying about seeing ghosts."

"Maybe you're the one who's lying," Julian said.

Celeste shoved him. "In case you forgot, idiot, I sensed ghosts first."

"Yeah, sensed them, not saw them. I saw them first. Years before you."

"Liar! You thought it was impressive, so you pretend to see them, too."

"I see them. They're everywhere. It's been that way for years." Julian rubbed his arms. "Why did we have to walk this way? You know the cemetery freaks me out."

"They're going to the cemetery?" Helen said.

"Because I'm in charge. What's the matter? Anyone would think you were afraid of ghosts." Celeste laughed and strode ahead of Julian.

The air around us chilled, and Lord Albert appeared. He floated along beside me, watching his children with a worried expression on his face.

"We've got ghostly company," I said to Helen. My gaze shifted to Lord Albert. "I expect you're not happy we're tailing your children, are you?"

He shook his head then shrugged as if accepting we needed to do this if we were going to help him.

"I know it must be hard to consider that either of them hurt you, but we must look at all the suspects. Celeste was in the dining room when you had your allergic reaction. And although Julian wasn't there all the time, he may have been able to put nuts in your food while it was in the kitchen."

Lord Albert shook his head at both suggestions, then waved and pointed at a small wooden gate.

"Oh! That's the cemetery." Helen was peering over the gate into the crisp expanse of grass, gravel paths, and headstones.

"Lord Albert wants us to go inside," I said.

"What about Celeste and Julian? We don't want to lose them."

Lord Albert jabbed a finger at the gate again, his gestures growing frantic.

"We can go in for a minute, if we're quick," I said.

Lord Albert zoomed ahead of us and stopped by a pristine white gravestone that looked like it hadn't long been in the ground. On top of it sat a single white rose.

"This is where he was laid to rest." Helen bent and inspected the grave.

Lord Albert nodded and pointed at the stone.

"It must be weird, seeing your own grave," Helen said. "If I had the chance to come back as a ghost, I wouldn't do it. It would be too freaky."

"Lord Albert doesn't have a choice but to stick around," I said. "He needs to find out what happened to him."

We stood in silence for a few seconds, the icy cold seeping through my coat.

"Who left the white rose?" Helen said.

"Maybe Lady Kate. Or one of the children." The petals were already icy as I touched the fragile flower.

"We should get going, or we'll have had a wasted journey if we don't find out what Celeste and Julian are up to," Helen said.

Lord Albert pointed at the grave again, and I nodded. "Don't worry. This will all be resolved soon. Thanks for showing us your final resting place."

He cast a sad look at the grave and disappeared.

We dashed along the frost spattered path until we caught sight of Julian and Celeste again.

"They're definitely going to the village," Helen said. "I see lights up ahead. This must be a shortcut only locals know about."

We hung back, and I couldn't help but feel disappointed about our destination. I wasn't certain what we'd find out by tailing them, but something as mundane as last-minute Christmas shopping hadn't been it.

It was easy enough to hide among the crowds of late-night shoppers as we watched Julian and Celeste. Celeste went into several stores, always coming out with a new bag, while Julian lingered outside. It seemed Celeste was the only one doing any shopping.

"They're splitting up," Helen said.

"I'll keep an eye on Celeste. You watch Julian," I said.

She wrinkled her nose. "Do I have to?"

"You were good with him in the café. And he's taken a shine to you. If he spots you, maybe he'll talk to you, rather than running off."

"I suppose I can use my feminine charm to stop him from panicking."

"I'll text you if I see Celeste getting up to anything she shouldn't."

"Ditto with Julian. See you soon." Helen hurried off after Julian.

I kept tabs on Celeste as she went into another three stores, spending ten minutes in each. I caught a glimpse of her in a couple of the stores, and she was smiling and laughing with the cashier and didn't seem to have a care in the world.

Part of me hoped I was wrong about Celeste. I liked her, but needed to be cautious. When her temper got out of control, she might not be safe to be around.

I sighed and tucked my coat around me, slowing to give Flipper a pet. Maybe this was a wild goose chase. Or maybe I shouldn't be deceived by Celeste's friendly smile and charm. Was she devious enough to plot a murder?

I was following her to another store when my phone buzzed. It was a message from Helen.

*Help!!! Cemetery. Now.*

# Chapter 14

My heart felt lodged in my throat as I raced back to the cemetery with Flipper. I tried calling Helen's phone, but she wasn't picking up.

I slipped on a patch of ice and landed hard on one knee, but didn't have time to think about the pain as I scrambled to my feet and dashed along the slippery path. Flipper ran ahead of me and straight through the cemetery gates.

"Find Helen," I yelled. "She's in trouble."

His ears pricked as he sniffed the freezing air.

There was a small bark followed by a squeak from somewhere in the cemetery. As I tried to locate the source, an ominous silence crept around me as a light spatter of freezing rain fell.

"Helen, where are you?"

There was no reply.

"Keep looking, Flipper. She's in here." The crunching of gravel under my boots sounded too loud as the silence from the graveyard made me shake with a mixture of fear and concern. An intense cold hit me, and a second later, Lord Albert appeared.

"Lord Albert! Have you seen Helen? She sent me a message saying she was in trouble."

He shook his head, concern crossing his face.

Flipper whined and nudged my hand with his nose.

I petted his head. "It's okay. We'll find her."

He nudged me again, and a second later, I was hit with a wave of dizziness that had me staggering back and hitting a headstone. I grabbed it before I fell.

Lord Albert was instantly by my side, trying to help me, but all he achieved was making me freezing as his ghostly hands passed through me several times.

As the dizziness grew intense, I realized what the problem was. More ghosts had appeared and were hovering nearby, their gazes fixed on me as if sensing my ghost whispering ability.

Flipper barked a warning, and his hackles rose as he stood in front of me to protect me from the ghosts.

"Lord Albert, help me out with these new arrivals. If there are too many ghosts around, I have an unhelpful habit of fainting, and I need to get to Helen."

Lord Albert pulled his shoulders back, then turned and zoomed over to the ghosts. Although I couldn't hear the conversation, it was clear he was telling them off from his gestures and fierce glare.

I tried to inch away, but every time I moved, the dizziness hit, so I clung to the headstone with one hand, my other on Flipper's head for comfort, and sucked in deep breaths. My gaze kept flicking around the cemetery, hoping I'd see Helen, but it was almost dark as the winter night drew in quickly, and I could barely see a thing.

I pulled out my phone and called Helen again. It went to voicemail, so I sent her a message. *We're in the cemetery. Where are you?*

Lord Albert ushered the other ghosts back, and once they were far enough away, I could stand without my knees buckling.

"Let's keep going, Flipper. Helen must be close. Sniff her out." I'd only gone a few steps before there was a grating sound from a pale gray mausoleum in the far corner of the cemetery.

I raced over to discover the large, heavy stone door was open. I switched to the torch function on my phone and shone it into the darkness. Helen was in one corner, and Julian stood in front of her.

Her frightened gaze flashed to me. "Be careful. Julian's angry."

I stepped inside and kept the light raised. "What's going on?"

Julian's wild-eyed gaze flicked to me, and he raised his hand. He was holding a large chunk of rock, and his palm was bleeding. "It's not safe. There's so much danger."

"Not from us." I eased through the gap, and Flipper followed, sticking close to my heels and softly growling as he spotted Julian had Helen trapped.

"They're everywhere. I can't get away from the ghosts. Why won't they leave me alone?" Julian's arm shook.

"I can help. But you need to let Helen go." My heart thundered so loudly, it made my ears ring.

"He won't listen to reason," Helen whispered. "I told him we want to help, but Julian doesn't believe me. He thinks I'm evil."

"You were following me. You're a spy," Julian yelled. "Do you work for the ghosts? They want to find out all about me so they can manipulate me. I knew you were too good to be real. You're a twisted angel in disguise."

"Helen's not an angel," I said.

"She is! She's too pretty to be real. Where are your wings? You're hiding them. Reveal your true form." Julian raised the rock.

Helen lifted her hands to shield herself. "Julian, stop! I'm not hiding anything from you."

Flipper growled again, and only my steadying hand on his head stopped him from attacking Julian.

"We were following you." I kept my tone soft. "We were worried about you being out with Celeste."

Julian's arm wavered, and he lowered the rock. "I don't know who to believe. Celeste was even being nice to me. Why would she do that, when she's usually so mean?"

"Maybe she feels bad about the way she treated you and is trying to make up for it," I said.

Helen inched away, but a glare from Julian froze her into place.

"I don't trust her. And I don't trust you two, either." Julian took a step toward Helen, and she squeaked.

Lord Albert shot into the mausoleum and stopped beside me, his gaze filling with shock as he saw what his son was doing.

Julian's gaze flashed to his dad, and he grimaced. "Why are you here? You should be gone. There's nothing good about you."

"What do you mean by that?" I said. "I know you weren't close to your dad, but you must have loved him."

Julian thumped a hand against the side of his head. "It wasn't him. Not at the end."

"Wasn't him? You've lost me," Helen said.

"Something... possessed my father. Before he died, his face changed. He looked evil. His eyes were too big for his head, and they glowed. I knew then that something unnatural had taken him. Ghosts are real, so why aren't demons, too? One of them pretended to be my dad, but I wasn't fooled."

Lord Albert appeared startled and gestured at Julian, trying to get him to understand him.

"When did you see this change?" I said.

"Just before Dad died," Julian said. "And it wasn't a one-off. I'd sometimes catch him watching other members of the family when he didn't think anyone was looking at him. He had evil on his mind. He wanted to hurt them, so he had to be stopped."

That almost sounded like a confession. "Julian, did you stop your dad from hurting other people?"

He groaned and shook his head. "I don't remember, but I knew he was a bad man. He wasn't even a man anymore. Darkness had taken over his soul. I couldn't let that thing live in the house."

"Did you give him the nuts?" Helen said. "You killed the demon?"

"Stop asking questions! I should never have trusted you two. I've told you too much. Now you're here to destroy me."

"No, Julian. We're just here to do our jobs and help your dad find out what happened to him," I said. "Think back to the night he died. Had you seen him looking evil that day?"

Julian was quiet for a long time, scuffing one foot back and forth across the stone floor. "My memories get muddled. I'm on strong medication for my anxiety. Whenever I mention ghosts, the doctor gets a condescending look on his face and supplies me with another pill to make everything go away. Pills don't work. I still see the ghosts and the bad things that lurk behind people's eyes. And those pills make me feel so sick and forgetful."

"I'm sorry to hear that," I said. "But try to think back to that evening when you had dinner with your dad. Did you go into the kitchen? Did you get your hands on some nuts and put them in your dad's food?"

"If I did, I don't remember." Julian took a step toward Helen, then backed away. "I don't know what I should do. I want this to stop."

"You were taking your medication then?" I said.

He shrugged. "Sure. I mean, sometimes. Mostly I take them."

"You hadn't stopped taking them that day?"

"I hate them. The pills get forced on me. They make me drowsy and queasy, and my skin itches. The only thing that calms me is being in the cold in wide-open spaces where I can run from the ghosts if they grab me."

Lord Albert moved closer to his son, but Julian cowered away from him.

"I don't trust you, either. You're not even my dad's ghost. You could be a demon in disguise. You're still trying to trick me. All of you are deceiving me."

"No, we want to help. You sound troubled, and that's unfair on you. Come with us. We'll go back to the house and talk," I said.

Julian shook his head. "Talking gets you nowhere. I've been in therapy for years, and it hasn't helped. I still see ghosts. I see the truth of this world. It's a hateful place."

"What's going on in here?" Celeste appeared in the open door of the mausoleum, clutching half a dozen bags. "Julian? I lost you. If I hadn't put that tracking app on your phone, I wouldn't have known where you were. What are you playing at?"

He pressed a hand over one ear. "They're making me say things."

"What are you doing to him?" Celeste marched over to her brother.

"Trying to help," I said. "Julian is troubled. He's admitted he thought something evil possessed Lord Albert."

Celeste rolled her eyes. "Pay no attention to him. He always has loopy ideas."

"Celeste, this is serious. Julian is worried he hurt your dad."

Her tart expression shifted, and she glanced at Lord Albert. "If he did, he didn't mean to do it.

Daddy, you know Julian is sensitive. It would have been an accident if he did something bad to you."

"You think he could have done it, though?" I said.

"I never said that." Celeste shot me a sharp look.

Lord Albert tried to pat his son's shoulder, but Julian dodged away, grimacing and shaking his head.

I was glad he'd moved, because it put some distance between him and Helen.

"Let's go home, idiot," Celeste said. "I'm tired. You can take your special pills and go to bed. Forget all about tonight. And everyone else must do the same. That is, if they want to keep their jobs."

"Julian doesn't like his pills," I said. "They make him feel sick."

"He has to take them. The doctors know best." Celeste tugged on Julian's arm. "Let's go. You can carry my bags. It'll keep you distracted from your fantasies."

I backed to the entrance of the mausoleum, Flipper matching my steps, until we blocked the way out. "Celeste, Julian needs help. Not just medical help, but he needs support from his family. You can both see ghosts, so you need to support him."

Her eyebrows rose. "What makes you think I'm not supporting him?"

"He's terrified of everything and everyone." I glanced at Helen and inclined my head to get her moving toward me. "We followed you this evening when you left home. You weren't being kind to your brother. If he's struggling, help him. You aren't scared of ghosts, so teach him how to behave around them."

She glowered at me. "Julian needs to learn these things for himself. Life is difficult. I experienced that when Daddy abandoned my sweet mother to be with Kate. I never got over that. We all have struggles."

"That's different to seeing ghosts, though."

Celeste huffed out a breath. "Seeing ghosts is my special thing. It's not fair other people claim to see them, too."

"You don't like it that I see ghosts?" I said.

She waved a bag-ladened arm at me. "You're different. You're so much older than me, and you'll be leaving soon. Julian has taken away my fun."

"If I remember right, he's been seeing ghosts longer than you."

She made a noise of disgust in the back of her throat. "So he reckons. He's always been a liar, though."

Julian's gaze flashed around the mausoleum. "The ghosts are speaking."

"Be quiet!" Celeste whacked him with a bag. "You see what I have to put up with? He's always showing off."

I tilted my head and listened. There was a faint whisper of something, but I couldn't catch a complete word. Julian really was attuned to the dead.

"You hear them, too?" His bright gaze was fixed on me.

I nodded, but kept my attention on Celeste.

Julian grabbed her arm. "I think I did it. I hurt Dad."

"You know no such thing. Everyone knows you're ill, but if you keep talking like that, you'll go to the hospital. You don't want that, do you? They'll stick you with needles and run horrible tests on you."

"Celeste, you're scaring him," I said. "The doctors will help if he needs it."

Julian shook from head to toe as he looked at his sister. "I hurt Dad. He was behaving strangely before he died. He was saying odd things, and his face kept changing. I had to stop him. I did it."

"Shush! Daddy was just the same as always. Be quiet in front of these people. We don't know them."

Julian pulled away and lunged. "Helen isn't real. She's too angelic."

Helen shrieked as Julian grabbed her.

Flipper and Milly attacked, Flipper leaping from my side and Milly out the top of Helen's coat. Flipper punched Julian in the chest with his paws, sending him to the floor, while Milly grabbed his arm and shook it, her tiny body shaking with rage that anyone had dared touch Helen.

"Stop! Don't hurt him." Although Celeste sounded frightened, she was smiling, looking like she was enjoying the fight.

"Flipper, hold," I said.

Flipper stamped his paws on Julian's chest and pinned him down. Milly kept hold of his arm.

"Helen, are you okay?" I asked.

She nodded as she smoothed down her hair and slowly stood. "I'm fine. Just shaken. Julian didn't hurt me."

Lord Albert zoomed around, looking frantic as he stared at his children.

I pulled out my phone.

"Wait! What are you going to do?" Celeste's smile slipped. "This was just fun. Julian wasn't being serious."

"Your brother just confessed to murder. I'm calling the police."

# Chapter 15

It took the police half an hour to get to the cemetery. And it took just that long again to explain the situation and why we were inside a mausoleum on a freezing cold night.

Julian had remained on the floor, curled into a ball and occasionally sobbing and saying he was sorry, while the police made sense of everything.

They'd naturally enough been surprised about the possibility Julian murdered his dad but accepted our explanation and, after consulting with colleagues, took Julian away for further questioning and, most likely, a psychiatric evaluation.

The police also contacted the rest of the Drew family, and we were just arriving back at the house to face what would be a difficult conversation.

"How do you think they'll take the news about Julian?" Helen muttered as we walked along the snowy, slippery driveway.

"It depends on what they've already heard from the police," I said.

"What about Celeste? She didn't stick around for long after the police questioned her."

"She must have come home. Celeste must know she needs to be with her family at this horrible time."

"You don't think she slunk off because she was feeling guilty?"

"Guilty about mistreating Julian?"

"Yes. If I'd not supported my vulnerable younger brother, and he'd just confessed to a murder, I'd feel like something I'd scraped off the sole of my boot. Poor Julian. He didn't stand a chance."

"Celeste wasn't helping when Julian spiraled, so he must feel so alone. I hope he gets the help he needs." I didn't like the outcome of this mystery. It felt wrong that someone so troubled was in such a grim situation.

"He's better off away from this family. Celeste seemed so nice when we met, but she only added to Julian's trauma. For all we know, she could have encouraged him to kill Lord Albert."

Before I replied, the front door of the house opened, and Lady Kate appeared. I increased my pace and met her by the door.

"Come in. I've been so worried since I received a call from the police. Tell me everything about Julian."

We followed her into the hallway, swiftly shrugging off our coats and boots. Helen hid Milly upstairs. Then we went into a cozy sitting room usually reserved for family members.

"What did the police tell you?" I said.

Lady Kate stood with her hands clenched. "Not much. They informed me Julian was taken in for questioning over my husband's death. They can't believe anything he has to say. He's very sick."

"We realize that," I said. "Julian cornered Helen in the cemetery this evening. He didn't think she was a real person. He tried to hurt her."

Lady Kate's gaze shot to Helen. "Were you injured?"

"No, we talked him down. But then he got upset again when Celeste arrived."

"Those two have never gotten along. Celeste's always been resentful of Julian. It got worse after his accident."

"When he fell off the yacht?" I said.

"Oh! Yes, how do you know about that?"

"Julian mentioned it. He said he's struggled since then."

"It started before that. He was a sensitive child, even from a young age," Lady Kate said. "But I can't believe he'd hurt his own father. They didn't have a close relationship, but there was no reason for him to do it."

Mary hurried into the room, with Annie closely following on her crutches. "We heard the news about Julian. Why didn't you come and tell me?" she asked Lady Kate.

"Because he's my son, and this is my business." Lady Kate's expression grew strained. "You don't need to be here."

"Kate, we've had our differences, but your child is in trouble. Of course, I want to help in any way I can." Mary looked over at us and nodded. "Annie was just telling me the news."

Annie rested on her crutches. "I've got a friend who works on the front desk at the local police station. She called when she saw Julian brought in. I was so shocked, I didn't know what to do."

"This is a private family matter," Lady Kate said. "Annie, you know better than to interfere."

"I'm sorry, but Lady Mary found me in shock and asked what was wrong. I didn't mean to gossip, but I was so surprised."

"Kate, let us help. You can't be alone at a time like this," Mary said.

The fight appeared to drain out of Lady Kate, and she sank onto the couch behind her. "I don't understand this. We had things under control."

Mary sat beside her, and Annie took the seat opposite. I remained standing with Helen and Flipper.

"Julian's been troubled for a long time," Mary said. "I know you never talk to me about it, but I have walked in on Julian crying and begging to be left alone. He'd never tell me what the problem was, but it was easy to see his distress."

Lady Kate dropped her head back and closed her eyes for a few seconds. "He's been having delusions for years. I've often wondered if the doctors missed something after his accident when he fell off the yacht."

"When he was pushed off by Celeste," Helen muttered to me.

"I never thought Julian was dangerous, though. So long as he takes his pills, he's fine," Lady Kate said.

Mary quietly cleared her throat and took one of Lady Kate's hands. "My dear, your son doesn't take his pills all the time."

Lady Kate stiffened in her seat and yanked her hand away. "How would you know that?"

"Because I've found the remains of them in the toilet bowl on several occasions. He flushes them away."

"Julian told us he doesn't enjoy taking his medication because it makes him sick and forgetful," I said.

"The pills have side effects, but they keep him calm, and they stop him from having those fantasies about ghosts and demons." Lady Kate glared at Mary. "Why didn't you tell me? I could have kept a closer eye on him and made sure he took his medicine."

"I wasn't certain what they were to begin with," Mary said. "One afternoon, he came out of the downstairs bathroom just before I went in. He rushed away and refused to speak to me. I found an empty pill pot beside the sink and dissolving pills in the toilet bowl. I mentioned it to Albert, and he said he'd speak to Julian. I thought everything was okay."

"Albert never thought there was anything wrong with Julian. But he wouldn't, since he spent so little time with our son. Celeste was always his favorite."

"He would still have looked after Julian," Mary said. "Albert loved him, even though they weren't close."

"It's too late to worry about that," Lady Kate said. "I'll make sure Julian gets the best medical help.

And I've already been on the phone with the family lawyer. He's going to the police station and will sit in on the interview. I want to be there, too, but Julian doesn't want to see anyone from the family."

"Then you've done everything you can for him," Mary said. "He'll be looked after and will get the right help."

Lady Kate looked over at me and Helen. "The police were vague on the phone about the evidence they had. Do you know anything? What was said to make them take him in for questioning?"

There was no easy way to break this news. "Julian thinks he may have put the nuts in Lord Albert's food."

Lady Kate's face drained of all color, and Mary gasped. Annie looked shocked as she reached over to clasp Lady Kate's shoulder.

"He admitted to it?" Her voice was strained.

"He did. Although Julian was confused. He's been seeing upsetting things and became convinced there was something wrong with Lord Albert."

"This is terrible," Lady Kate said. "What if the police get a confession when he doesn't know what he's saying? It will ruin him."

"Your lawyer won't allow that," Mary said. "You've got the best in the business helping. Let them do their jobs, and Julian will be out in time to celebrate Christmas."

"Oh my goodness, Christmas! The Winter Wonderland Gala. I should cancel. With everything going on, it doesn't seem right to have a big party." Lady Kate's anxious gaze flicked around the room.

"But it's only a few days away," Annie said. "I'm not sure we can cancel everything at such short notice. And... Julian will get out. I'm sure of it."

Lady Kate looked so helpless as she stared at the wall. "I don't know what to do."

"That's where we can help. And we'll do whatever we have to do to ensure you have nothing to worry about with the gala," I said. Lady Kate didn't need to worry about canapes and guest lists.

"Don't cancel just yet," Mary said. "Julian could be out in a few hours, and this will have blown over."

"What if they charge him with Albert's murder?" Lady Kate said. "It wouldn't look right to have a celebration while my son is in jail."

"Let's wait until the morning," I said. "We'll know more then."

Lady Kate sighed, then nodded. "I'll keep things as they are for now. But I can't think about a party with this hanging over my head."

"I agree with Lorna. Even if you decide to cancel, we can't do anything until the morning," Annie said. "All the companies will have closed for the night."

I nodded. "Although I'm sure the businesses will understand. I expect a few will be pleased they don't need to travel out this far, since the weather is so bad."

"Very well. I'll try to be positive and contact the police again in an hour. I just want Julian home." Lady Kate hid her face in her hands.

"We should leave you to it," I said.

"Thank you. Sorry for what happened this evening with Julian." Lady Kate lifted her head, her eyes bright with unshed tears. "He's not malicious, but as you've discovered, he has demons he's struggling with."

"Of course. We understand," Helen said. "And he didn't hurt me. I was just startled by his behavior."

"Have any of you seen Celeste?" Mary said. "I've been trying to get hold of her to make sure she's okay, but she's not answering her phone."

"She was with us in the cemetery but left before we did," I said. "Celeste didn't say where she was going. I assumed she came back here."

"If she has, I haven't seen her," Mary said. "Perhaps she's gone to the police station to see how Julian is doing."

"Your daughter would hardly be helping my son. She's a part of his problems," Lady Kate said.

"You would say that." Mary stood from her seat, her expression tight. "But Julian is twice as bad as Celeste, as we've just discovered."

"Why don't I make some soothing mugs of chamomile tea?" Helen said rapidly as the tension grew. "And there are fresh triple chocolate and cranberry brownies in the kitchen. Everyone needs something to help them relax after the shock of this evening."

Mary gave a curt nod. "I'll take mine in my room, if it's not too much trouble."

I was glad Helen had intervened. The last thing we needed was another family argument erupting.

"Not a problem. I'll go make the tea." Helen nudged me with an elbow and gestured her head at the door.

"I'll stay here with Lady Kate," Annie said.

I nodded my approval then walked out with Mary and Helen and eased the door shut.

Mary blew out a slow breath and rubbed her forehead. "I didn't mean to snap, but everyone's nerves are frayed. Kate can never leave it alone. She's always finding someone else to blame for her problems. Of course, Celeste isn't involved in making Julian worse."

"Why don't you go up to your room?" I said. "And try not to worry. I'm sure Celeste will be back soon."

"Yes, I think I will. I'm so grateful you and Helen are here. You defused an awkward situation." Mary turned and headed up the stairs.

After helping Helen with the brownies and chamomile tea and getting everyone settled in, we retreated to the kitchen. Although I had no plans to relax, since we needed to talk about murder.

Helen brought out a tray of mini chocolate yule logs, sweet cranberry tarts, and hot chocolate and set them in front of me on the table. "We deserve these. What an evening. I was almost killed in a mausoleum. What kind of Christmas gift would that have been for Gunner?" She sank into a chair.

"We were lucky you got away with only being scared by Julian. He was out of control for a minute."

"It's also lucky I'm a speedy texter, and you and Flipper are fast, or I'd have been toast." She bit into a tart. "Weren't our dogs brave? I'll have to reward Milly for protecting me. And Flipper."

"I can't help feeling this victory is hollow. A damaged young man got in trouble because he didn't get the help he needed. It's tragic."

Flipper raised his head and whined, just as Lord Albert floated through the door.

"Lord Albert's here," I said to Helen, "and he's not looking happy."

He shook his head as he drifted around the table.

"It looks like we found your killer," I said. "I know it won't be much comfort, but at least you know what happened."

He shook his head again.

"You don't feel ready to move on?"

"You can hardly blame him," Helen said. "This evening has been one big mess."

Flipper jumped up and followed Lord Albert around the kitchen as he swirled about, dropping the temperature by several degrees.

"Please, try to relax," I said to him. "I know you've had a stressful evening, but you're worrying my dog."

"And making my nose cold," Helen said.

Lord Albert looked down at Flipper and slowly drifted to the door, where he stayed still.

Flipper raised a paw and whined again before he turned in a circle and walked to the back door.

"Take Flipper outside," Helen said. "That will calm him down. You can take Lord Albert too if you like. The kitchen is freezing. I'll need more hot chocolate to warm up."

I grinned at her. "Any excuse."

She returned my grin. "You'll get one, too. And I'll add some mini marshmallows on the top."

I looked over at Lord Albert, but he simply shook his head and slowly faded. "It's going to take Lord Albert a while to accept what happened."

"The poor man. Killed by one of his children. It won't be a fun Christmas for him."

"Or anyone left behind as they come to terms with what happened." I grabbed a mini chocolate yule log sprinkled with icing sugar. "I'll be quick. I'll take Flipper out to do his business, and he should settle after that."

"Don't be long. It's cold out there," Helen said.

I grabbed my coat and boots then hurried into the crisp, frosty night. The icy rain that had been falling had turned to snow, and it slowly drifted around us as we walked, Flipper sniffing about to find the perfect spot.

My head tilted as I heard someone talking. It was a woman's voice, soft, low, and close by.

I crept to the corner of the building and poked my head around the side. It was Lady Kate on her phone, standing near the front door of the house with her head down.

I gestured at Flipper to stay back, but he was content to sniff around and not reveal us as I listened to the conversation.

"It is difficult. But we'll be together soon," Lady Kate said.

Who was she talking to?

"It won't be long. Give me a little time to smooth things over." There was a pause as she listened to the other side of the conversation.

"Yes. I love you, too. Goodbye."

With my heart thundering, I tiptoed away. Had Lady Kate been seeing someone behind Lord Albert's back? Was she planning on leaving so she could be with her lover?

With possibilities filling my head, I realized this mystery wasn't over yet.

# Chapter 16

I flipped over the page of planning notes I'd been attempting to digest for what felt like the tenth time. I pushed back from the desk and closed my eyes. I hadn't been able to focus on the Winter Wonderland Gala since Julian's arrest. And I kept replaying the conversation I'd overheard last night. Who had Lady Kate been talking to? I couldn't be certain she was in a relationship with someone behind Lord Albert's back, but from the tone of her voice, she hadn't been talking to a friend.

Work! I had to focus on work. The big event was speeding toward me like an out-of-control Santa sleigh, and I had to make sure everything went smoothly. Of course, there was a chance the whole thing would be canceled, but until I knew that for certain, I needed to focus.

I checked my phone and frowned. Helen had been up before me this morning, and I'd looked everywhere for her, so I could only assume she'd left the house on another one of her secret missions. And she wasn't returning my text messages or phone calls. I wanted to talk to her about my concerns over Julian's arrest and his confession again and run through the mysterious call I overheard one more time. But first, I needed to find her.

The door creaked open, and Annie shuffled in on her crutches. "Hey, how's everything going?"

I looked at the plans. "So far, so slowly. I'm having trouble concentrating."

"It's no surprise." Annie eased into a seat and set her crutches to one side. "After everything that happened yesterday, I wouldn't be surprised to see you pack your bags and leave."

"No, we're not ready to go just yet. Not while everything is so up in the air." And especially not while I had questions lingering over what really happened to Lord Albert.

"That's good of you. How's Helen feeling?"

"If I could find her, I'd ask her."

"She is okay, though? You don't think she's gone to see the doctor, do you?"

"Oh! I didn't think about that. She was fine last night, but maybe she didn't feel well this morning." I looked at my phone. She should be able to reply to me, even if she was at the doctor's getting checked out.

"Sorry, I didn't mean to concern you. I'm sure Helen's fine. Perhaps she had a job that needed to be done early. After all, the Winter Wonderland event isn't far away."

"Do you think it'll still go ahead?" I tapped my fingers on the desk. Now I was worried about Helen, Lord Albert, and the event.

"I think so. Although I'm not sure how Lady Kate will feel if Julian is charged with Lord Albert's murder."

"She'll feel awful and won't think it appropriate to have a party when her son is in jail."

"Let's hope it doesn't come to that. Julian is a sweet boy, despite his troubles. I didn't know him until after he'd had his fall off the yacht, but everyone said he was a charming little boy. Very bright."

Flipper raised his head, and his gaze went to the door just as Lord Albert floated through. He nodded at me, his expression showing how miserable he felt.

"Shall I get started on opening the mail?" Annie said. "I'm feeling better today, and my ankle isn't hurting, so I can help you for a couple of hours."

"Thanks. That would be great." I edged my phone across the desk, so Lord Albert could use it if he wanted to.

He drifted over and spent a couple of minutes jabbing at the phone.

While Annie was distracted by opening the post, I looked at his message.

*Not Julian.*

I lifted my shoulders and raised my eyebrows at him. Julian's confession suggested otherwise.

Flipper trotted around the office as Lord Albert floated about in a distracted manner. He returned to the phone and struggled over it, jabbing away again, his frustration growing, as he couldn't type out what he wanted to tell me.

I glanced at the phone again.

*Why so sneaky?*

I checked Annie was still busy before taking the phone and typing in my reply. *So he could get away with killing you?*

Lord Albert dismissed that comment with a wave of his hand, and I tutted.

"Lorna, is everything okay?"

I looked over to see Annie studying me with a cautious expression on her face.

"Everything's good. Like I said, I keep getting distracted."

"There's nothing we can do to help Julian or anyone else right now." Annie rubbed her arms. "Maybe if it was warmer in here, you'd be able to concentrate better. These old places leak heat, although this room is usually cozy. I can get one of the staff to light a fire."

The reason for the cold was apparent as Lord Albert drifted about, leaving a trail of chilliness and gloom everywhere he went. Flipper remained by his side, seeming to sense the ghost's misery and wanting to help.

"A fire would be good. I'll go find someone to lay it. I'd do it myself, but I can never get it right, and smoke ends up billowing into the room."

"I'm good with fires, but right now, I'm struggling to stay upright if I do anything as strenuous as brush my teeth." She pointed to her leg and shook her head. "I can't wait until I'm properly back on my feet again. I used to run, and I miss the exercise."

"Not in the snow, though."

"All year round. I'm no fair weather jogger."

"Any news about your surgery?"

"Not yet. I should hear soon. I've got another doctor's appointment coming up. I'm hoping the Christmas fairies will sprinkle their magic over my injury, and it'll get better without surgical intervention."

"Make sure that wish is at the top of your Christmas list."

"I will." Annie finished checking through the mail. "Most of this isn't important. I'll file it away then get to work on some admin for the event."

I glanced at the list of things to do, but I wasn't in the right frame of mind to work. "Should I check in with Lady Kate? See how things are with Julian?"

"She's not here. She was up at dawn. Most likely went to see Julian."

"Maybe Lady Kate got a call from the police. I don't suppose you could check with your friend at the station to see if there's any news, could you?"

"Already on it. I sent a text this morning and am just waiting to hear back. She doesn't start work until nine, though, so she won't be able to tell me anything until then." Annie gathered up the post, collected her crutches, and limped to the other side of the office.

"Lorna, I'm glad you're in here. I'm exhausted, and I must have someone to talk to." Celeste strode into the room and over to the desk where I sat. "Daddy had me up most of last night worrying about Julian. He kept saying it wasn't him. He's innocent, and this is all a mistake. You can get through to him. You must tell him to stop."

"Um... Now's not a great time." I nodded my head in Annie's direction, but Celeste carried on.

"He was floating around, making the room freezing and insisting it wasn't Julian who gave him those nuts. I tried to reason with him, but he wasn't in the mood to listen. And he wouldn't let me sleep. What was I supposed to do in the middle of the night? Start questioning everyone whether they put nuts in Daddy's food? You have to finish this. Too many sleepless nights, and I'll look haggard."

Lord Albert whizzed over and waved his hands in front of Celeste's face.

"I'm not talking to you, Daddy," Celeste said. "I'm tired, and I have big circles under my eyes. That's your fault. You'd better not do that again. I need to look my best for the Winter Wonderland Gala."

"Good morning, Celeste." Annie hobbled back to her desk.

Celeste whirled around. "Oh! I didn't know you were in here."

"It's not a surprise Annie's here. She does work in this office," I said.

"Were you saying something about Lord Albert?" Annie said, even though she must have heard every word that came out of Celeste's mouth.

"No. I mean, yes. It's nothing." Celeste waved a hand about.

"It sounds like you were having some vivid dreams last night." I wasn't sure if my attempt to cover up Celeste's outburst would work, but I had to try something.

"Dreams? Yes, that's what I was having. I mean, I should go. I need breakfast." Celeste hurried out of the room in a whirlwind of indignation and annoyance.

Lord Albert looked at me and shook his head before floating after his daughter.

Annie moved to my desk and leaned against it. "I like Celeste and Julian, but they're both odd. I blame it on them watching too many haunted house shows when they were young. Things like that stick with children."

"Maybe it's that. They do have vivid imaginations."

Annie glanced at the door. "I never say anything in front of Lady Kate, but I find it creepy that they talk to themselves. Julian more than Celeste. Whenever I hear him, he sounds afraid. He's often asking to be left alone. I even questioned him about it, but he wouldn't say what was bothering him."

"He does seem very sensitive."

Annie glanced around the room. "Sometimes I think it would be easier to believe they see spirits, or ghosts, or whatever you want to call them. Celeste often sounds like she's having conversations with Lord Albert, just like she did then."

"You'd find it less spooky if ghosts were real?"

Her laugh sounded full of nerves. "Maybe not. But at least it would mean Celeste and Julian weren't unwell. Julian is getting help, but as for Celeste, I'm hoping it's a phase."

"As long as it's not doing anyone harm, I don't see why either of them should stop talking to ghosts. Real or not."

Annie grimaced. "It's dark, though. And it doesn't make Julian happy. He spends most of his life looking terrified. Did you know he'd been sectioned before?"

"I didn't. What happened to him?"

"It was before my time, so I only heard it through the local gossip. Emma, the cook who used to work here, told me, and I trust her."

"I've met her a couple of times. She seems nice."

"I think so. Emma said Julian was sent away for several months, not long after his accident. He was having night terrors and seeing things that weren't there. The doctor wondered if he'd sustained brain damage. He was in the water for a while and stopped breathing for a short time. Apparently, since then, he's been different." Annie pursed her lips. "Maybe it would be better for him to be in the hands of the professionals if he's struggling. Especially if his illness led him to kill Lord Albert."

"It could be for the best. I feel so sorry for him and the whole family."

"After learning what Julian almost did to Helen, it reminded me of a few times I've been uneasy around him. And if he's not taking his medication anymore..." Annie lifted her shoulders and let the unspoken truth linger.

"Julian is struggling. But I'm sure Lady Kate will do the best for him."

"Me, too. Although sometimes I think she's wanted to give up. Having a troubled child must be stressful."

While Annie was in a chatty mood, I pressed to see if I could find out about Lady Kate's secret relationship. "I suppose Lady Kate must be considering her future."

Annie's eyebrows flashed up. "I think she's only focused on Julian at the moment."

"Of course. But she's an attractive woman, and I'm sure she'll have her fair share of interest now she's single again."

"Oh! You're thinking about her dating? It's too soon. She's still getting over Lord Albert."

"They were happy together, though?" I said. "You never thought Lady Kate wasn't content in the marriage? There was a big age gap between them."

"Not that I know of. Although they spent little time together. They were busy people. Lord Albert was semi-retired but still worked a couple of days a week and had his charitable projects he like to spend time with. That wasn't Lady Kate's thing. They had different interests and hobbies. It kept them apart. But I don't think the age gap was an issue," Annie said. "I prefer older guys, too. Guys my age are immature. They still want to go drinking with the lads and not tidy up after themselves because they think their mom will do it."

"That's true. And I suppose the money and big house helped smooth over the age difference."

Annie smiled. "You cynic. Don't you believe in true love?"

"Absolutely. I just think some people fall more easily into love when there's lots of money on the table."

"Maybe. It was probably a bonus to the marriage. But Lady Kate came into the relationship with her own assets, so it wasn't the only reason they got married." Her gaze flicked to the window. "That's the car. Lady Kate must be back."

We walked to the window, and my eyes widened as the back door opened and Julian climbed out.

"He's been released," Annie said. "Lady Kate must have pulled a few strings to make that happen so fast. I was certain I wouldn't see Julian again."

"I'll see what's going on." I hurried into the hallway just as the front door opened. Julian raced past, not sparing me a glance, and sped up the stairs.

Lady Kate was close behind him. A man in a dark overcoat, smart black suit, and a crisp white shirt accompanied her.

"Lorna, did you see which way Julian went?" she asked.

"Upstairs. I'm glad you got him released."

She nodded then glanced at the man beside her. "This is our family lawyer, Nathaniel Barker. He made sure Julian was released without charge."

"That's great news." I nodded at Nathaniel. "Does that mean he's no longer a suspect?"

Lady Kate shook her head. "Sadly not. The police are still investigating. And Julian didn't follow my guidance about not talking. He's gotten himself in trouble."

"I'll make things right." Nathaniel shrugged off his large winter coat. "The police only have his word for what happened that night, and he's already changed his story several times. Once the doctor has examined him, things will swing in our favor."

I wanted to ask more questions, but Lady Kate appeared flustered and anxious, her gaze on the stairs.

"I'm sure you're right. Lorna, you and Helen take the day off. I need to focus on Julian. I can't think about anything else," Lady Kate said.

"Of course. If there's anything we can do to help, just ask."

"That's good of you." She moved to the bottom of the stairs then paused. "And I think, for now, we'll keep things as they stand with the gala, but don't do any more work on it. Tell Annie the same. I should know more in the next day or so. Nathaniel, make yourself at home. You know where everything is." Lady Kate hurried up the stairs.

Nathaniel looked at me, his gaze appraising. "I heard you and your friend were involved in an altercation with Julian prior to his confession and arrest in the cemetery."

"Not so much an altercation. He startled Helen, but we talked him down."

"You heard him make the confession about killing his father?"

"Yes, but he was confused, and I'm not certain Julian knew what he was telling us."

"Don't pay any attention to his comments and say nothing to the police. We're on top of things. Now, if you'll excuse me." Nathaniel marched away to the kitchen.

I went back to the office, let Annie know we weren't needed for the rest of the day, and filled her in on Julian's release. After she'd hobbled away, there was nothing left to do, so I took Flipper for a walk.

He bounded around, jumping in the snow and chasing snowballs I threw for him. I didn't want to be out for long because it was cold, so I decided a few circuits around the house and front yard would be enough, before heading inside for a warming breakfast. Then I'd look for Helen again.

We'd started the second circuit around the house and had just gotten around the back when the sound of a window sliding open had me looking up.

A second later, Julian appeared in the window and threw himself out.

# Chapter 17

Flipper's anxious bark masked my cry of horror as Julian plummeted to the ground, his arms flapping as if trying to fly.

I raced toward him, almost too scared to look for fear of the gruesome sight I'd discover.

Flipper bounded ahead, leaping over a huge snowdrift and disappearing from sight.

"Julian! Where are you? Make a sound if you can hear me." I had my phone in my hand, trying to dial for an ambulance, but my fingers were too numb and wouldn't cooperate.

The snow grew thicker as I approached the spot where Julian had landed, and I was soon wading through clumps of freezing snow up to my knees. Although I couldn't see Flipper, I could hear him whining.

I scrambled over the final pile of snow and sucked in a breath. Julian was on his back, his eyes open. He turned his head and blinked at me.

"You're alive!" I looked up at the window. He'd fallen four stories.

Julian gently pushed Flipper away and sat up. "I hoped the snow would be soft enough to cushion the fall."

"You weren't trying to..." I pointed up at the window. "Did you mean to hurt yourself?"

Julian rolled over and stood. He shook out each arm and leg. "You think I was trying to top myself? It's crossed my mind, especially after last night, being stuck with the police. But no, I just needed to get out of the house. Dad's ghost won't leave me alone, and Mom keeps knocking on the door and asking if there's anything she can do. I couldn't stand it. I need to be on my own."

Flipper licked Julian's hand, and Julian crouched and stroked Flipper's head.

"You're sure you aren't hurt?" I said. "That was a big fall. And a huge risk."

"I'm a bit winded, but I'll be fine." Julian looked back at the house. "I have to get out of here, though. The place is too claustrophobic. I need time to think."

Lord Albert swirled out the window Julian had fallen from and stopped in front of his son. Horror was written all over his face as he jabbed a finger at him and silently ranted.

Julian cringed away. "Dad, please, leave me alone. You're making things worse."

Lord Albert jabbed a finger at me, and it took me a few seconds to realize he wanted the phone I still clutched. I swiped the snow off the window ledge before setting it down.

Lord Albert jabbed at it.

"What's he doing?" Julian said.

"It's how we communicate. Like you, I don't hear ghosts, but Celeste figured out your dad can use the messaging app. Although he needs to concentrate. It takes a lot of energy."

"Sometimes, I do hear the ghosts talking," Julian said. "They mainly scream or beg. It's horrible. Why can't they talk to me like a normal person? Well, a normal ghost. It's like they've watched the worst horror movies and are reenacting them for me."

"They could be doing it out of frustration. I occasionally hear screams but rarely words. Maybe you could communicate with your dad using your phone, like I do. It's slow going, but it's not frightening."

I checked the phone. The message read: *Help him. He's imp.*

I tilted my head. "Julian's an imp?"

Julian smirked. "He probably means innocent. I wish."

I looked at Lord Albert. Of course, he'd want to protect his son, even if Julian had done something bad to him. "Maybe you have to accept things went wrong for Julian."

Julian looked at the message again and shrugged. "I wish I could say I didn't do it, but I don't remember much about the evening Dad died."

I gently gestured for Lord Albert to move away. "Let's go somewhere and talk. Just the two of us and Flipper. No ghosts allowed."

"If you can chase away the ghosts, I'll agree to anything," Julian said.

I gave Lord Albert a pointed look. "If any ghosts come our way, I'll send them off. And that includes you, Lord Albert. Your son needs some quiet time. I'm sure you understand."

He didn't look happy, but after a few seconds, he drifted back inside the house.

"We should move," I said. "I don't expect your mom will leave you alone for long. When she discovers your room is empty, she'll come looking for you."

"She's so overprotective. I never get a break. If she isn't pestering me, my dad is, or Celeste is poking fun at me and telling me I'm a weirdo."

"Let's get out of here. Where would you like to go?"

He thought for a second. "Have you been to Bluff Point?"

"No. Is it close by?"

"We'll need a car, but it's only a twenty-minute drive."

I hesitated. It wasn't the safest of ideas to go anywhere with Julian on my own, not after last night.

"You think I'm weird, too," Julian said with a sigh. "I get it. I'm used to it. If it's any help, I took my meds yesterday. I didn't have a choice while in police custody. I'm feeling stable for the first time in a while."

"Let's go to Bluff Point, then." I sent a quick message to Helen to let her know where I was going. I also had Flipper with me, and he'd protect me from any danger.

I grabbed keys from the cabinet in the kitchen, left a note to say I'd borrowed a car, and headed out and picked up Julian and Flipper. I'd also thrown in a warm coat for Julian and some snacks.

We drove mainly in silence, other than Julian giving me directions. The drive took us uphill, and the roads were slippery, but I took it slowly, and we made it into a large woodland clearing with a stunning view over the Berkshire countryside.

"Wow! You can see for miles." The stark, icy fields looked eerily beautiful, dressed in their winter coats of snow and ice.

"Yeah, it's pretty decent up here. And don't get freaked out, but this is a local make out point." Julian grinned at me. "All the cool kids hang out here with their girlfriends."

I arched an eyebrow at him. "Is that so?"

He looked away, his cheeks flushing pink. "I've never brought anyone here, but that's what I heard."

"It's a beautiful spot. I can understand why you like it. And it's peaceful."

"It is. Let's take a walk." Julian climbed out.

I hurried to join him and opened the back door, so Flipper could get out, too. We walked around for a few minutes, not talking. I gave Julian space and time to gather his thoughts. I could tell by the concentration lines on his forehead he was figuring things out. Or trying to.

"You'd think, living in a big house and having no money worries, life would be so easy." His voice was quiet as he looked out over the countryside.

"I've worked in a few big homes with wealthy families, so I know that's not true," I said.

"You've seen other people struggle?"

"Every family has its struggles. Some put on a brave face, but behind closed doors, there were problems. And money can cause complications. People don't know what to do with it, or they invest it badly, or someone wants to take it from them. Money doesn't always buy happiness."

"I'd give it all away, if it meant I never saw ghosts again," Julian said. "How do you manage it? You're so composed around Dad."

"It wasn't easy to begin with. Much like you, I was scared. There were times when I didn't know what was a ghost and what was a real person, especially to begin with. I've even lost jobs because I got caught talking to ghosts. Well, people would see me talking to thin air and assume the worst about me."

"That's happened to me. The getting-caught-talking-to-nobody part," Julian said. "I get lost in the conversations when trying to convince the ghosts to leave me alone. Then I hear someone behind me, and they're watching me like I've lost my mind."

"Things changed for me once I got Flipper," I said. "I don't know if ghosts have the same effect on you, but I get dizzy."

"Yeah, really dizzy. And I sometimes feel sick, too."

"When I found Flipper, I realized he was special. He senses ghosts. He knows when one is coming and can see them. He's my protector. When I go to a new job, I tell people he's my assistance dog. And he's wonderful. He's my early warning system for ghosts."

"Huh! I don't suppose you want to give him to me, do you?" Julian said. "It would be amazing to have a ghost alarm."

"I can't do that. He's my fur baby. But maybe we can find you your own Flipper."

"I doubt it." Julian stubbed his toe on the ground. "Flipper sounds like one of a kind."

"Lots of animals are sensitive to ghosts. We could go to the local shelter and see if there are any suitable for you. I'm sure your dad won't mind coming along and helping. If any dogs see him, that would be a good way to start. And I know an amazing animal shelter close by. They'd be thrilled if you adopted a dog."

"I guess. I won't be able to keep a dog if I get charged with my dad's murder, though."

"He thinks you're innocent."

"But I confessed to you and Helen. How can I take that back?"

"Simple. Julian, you haven't been taking your medication. I know little about the drugs you're on, but they sound strong. It must be easy to get confused if you get your prescriptions muddled or miss a few days."

He heaved out a sigh and shoved his hands into his pants pockets. "I wish I didn't have to take them. I want to get used to being around ghosts, but every time I try, it's overwhelming. Sometimes, I want to give up."

"Don't do that. You're not alone. I hope it comforts you to know there are other people who see ghosts, too. Your sister, included."

"She's no help. I can't stand Celeste. She's a bully. I wish I had a nice sister, like you."

"That's sweet of you. But if I was your actual sister, I'd have been just as annoying. That's what siblings do to each other."

"Maybe. It is good to know I'm not such a freak."

"We can be freaks together," I said. We walked along a path overlooking the striking view. "Are you willing to talk about the night of your dad's death? Maybe discussing it will make things clearer."

"I talked it through with the police several times last night. All it did was get me confused and angry."

"How about you talk, and I listen?"

He glanced at me. "Do you think you can do that?"

I chuckled. "I'll do my best to keep it zipped."

Julian looked away again and stopped walking. Flipper moved over and leaned against his leg, and Julian petted him as he gathered his thoughts. "I'm having doubts I had anything to do with my dad's murder. I was around that evening but was feeling bad. I couldn't remember what pills I'd taken and was scared, if I took the wrong ones or too many, I'd get ill. One of the pills always makes me feel like the walls are closing in on me. Have you ever felt like that?"

"No, but it sounds awful."

"It makes it hard to breathe. It's why I go outside a lot. When I can see clearly all around me, it helps. Anyway, it was dinnertime, and I felt ready to explode. I'd been feeling like something big was building all day. I've mentioned there are other ghosts in the house, haven't I? I forget what I've told you."

"You have. Although I've never seen them."

"They don't come out much. Most of them just drift around, but there's one old lady who is always screaming. She'd been bothering me most of the day, and I had a throbbing headache. I showed my face at dinner so my parents wouldn't nag me, but the next thing I remember, I was outside." His gaze shot my way. "I don't think I did it, though, even though I didn't have a great relationship with my dad. He didn't understand what I was going through. And my mood swings bothered him. Maybe, that evening, I tipped to the dark side and blanked it out."

"You don't remember for sure what you did?"

He grinned at me. "Is that you keeping it zipped?"

I raised my hands. "Sorry. I can't help myself. It sounds to me like you're not sure. Have you told the police?"

"Yeah, several times. With Mom's help and the lawyer, they got me out because I wasn't making much sense. I heard an officer mutter I was making it up, though. I'm not. This seems to be my life, these days. I'm always unsure." Julian turned and stared me straight in the face. "Lorna, I know I scared you and Helen last night, but I need help. Not with pills, but from someone who knows what I'm going through. If I did this, I have to know for sure. And if I didn't, I need to know who killed my dad."

Flipper whined and licked Julian's hand again.

"Helen and I know you didn't deliberately mean to scare us. And Helen is fine. All is forgiven." My gaze traveled over Julian. I was conflicted about helping him, but there was so much doubt and uncertainty in his confession. And the haunted look in his eyes made my heart sad for him.

"You can see my dad, and you're trying to help him. Whatever happens, I'll accept the outcome," Julian whispered. "If I did this, I won't fight the police. I'll take my punishment."

"That's a mature response to a chaotic situation."

"I can be sensible when I have to be," Julian said. "And we're away from the house, the ghosts, and all the stress, so I already feel better."

I nodded as I made my decision. I'd keep looking at the other suspects. I wasn't prepared to accept this unhappy ending to Lord Albert's mystery. We may need Christmas magic to help solve this, but I wasn't done yet.

"We should get back to the house," I said. "Your mom will be worrying."

He groaned. "Ten more minutes."

"Okay. But when we get back, how about I have a word with your mom? I could say you've talked to me and asked for a quiet day on your own to think things through. Would that help?"

"That would be great. And I'll be as normal as I can when I'm back, so she doesn't freak out."

"You be you, ghost seeing abilities and all. You'll have a few struggles, but I'm around, and I'll help with any questions you have about ghosts. Think of me as your unofficial mentor, if you like. And if you don't want me around, tell me to get lost. I won't take it personally. I know how draining the ghosts can be. Did you know, they take energy from us, so they grow stronger?"

"No. But it makes sense. I feel exhausted when I've spent the day hiding from one." Julian shifted his weight from foot to foot. "Thanks. I'm glad you and Helen came to work here. The mood already feels different. And I feel more hopeful for the future."

"That's what everyone needs, a little hope. Never give up looking for the truth." And I desperately wanted to know the truth about what happened to Lord Albert. But I wasn't sure how I'd figure that out.

# Chapter 18

After driving back to the house with Julian, I stopped the car and turned to him.

He lifted a hand. "I'm good. Thanks. I've got a lot to think about."

"You know where I am if you need me."

He nodded, hopped out of the car, and headed across the front yard, giving me a wave as he went inside.

It seemed our conversation had lightened his mood, and I was glad. I hated seeing anyone struggling. And I liked to think I'd eased his burden. I might ease it even more if I could figure out who actually killed his dad.

I tucked the car back in the garage and was walking back to the front door when I slowed. That was Zach's voice. He couldn't be back here again so soon, could he?

I checked my phone to see if I'd missed a message from him, but there was nothing. There were also no replies from the numerous messages I'd left Helen.

A familiar giggle reached my ears, and I frowned. Helen was with Zach?

I wasn't close enough to hear their conversation, but I wasn't the only one who'd recognized the voices. Flipper's ears pricked, and he raced off, despite me hiss-whispering for him to come back.

It was one of the few times he ignored me, because wherever Zach was, his dog, Jessie wasn't far behind, and Flipper adored her. Nothing I could say would convince him to return.

"Flipper! What are you doing out here on your own?" Zach's tone was full of surprise.

I remained where I was, chewing on my lip and wondering what to do.

Flipper's replying bark was happy, and I could imagine Zach bending to pet him and feed him a treat from the supply he kept in his coat pocket.

I couldn't decide whether to remain hiding or march around the side of the building and ask Zach what he was doing with Helen. Not that I didn't trust them together, but why would Zach show up and not let me know he was in the area? And what was with Helen's secret conversations and her disappearing act? These things were connected, but I couldn't figure out how.

Footsteps crunching over the gravel had me ducking behind a bush. Until I knew what was going on, I didn't want to confront anyone.

A swirl of coldness bit into my back, and I turned to see Lord Albert staring at me with confusion in his eyes.

I pressed a finger to my lips.

He gestured at me to get inside the house, but I shook my head. I didn't want to be seen by Helen and Zach listening to their conversation.

He kept gesturing at me until I pulled my phone out and held it for him to use.

It took him about five minutes to type a short message, and all the time I was waiting, I kept checking to see if Zach or Helen had noticed me. But they stayed out of sight.

Lord Albert moved back and pointed at the phone. *Solve murder.*

"That's what I'm doing," I whispered. "My conversation with Julian was useful. I don't think he did it."

Lord Albert nodded vigorously.

"Which means, we need to keep looking at the other suspects."

He pointed at the house.

"Yes! But I've got my own things going on."

Lord Albert tilted his head.

"It's complicated. And I don't fully understand it." What was my fiancé and best friend up to that meant I wasn't allowed to be involved?

An engine started, and I recognized the familiar rumble of Zach's Jeep. He was leaving without seeing me? I waited another minute, then pulled back my shoulders and walked around to the front of the house.

Helen was going in through the front door. She turned at the sound of me approaching, and her gaze flashed to the driveway, where Zach's Jeep must have just been. "Oh, there you are. I saw Flipper, so I figured you weren't far behind."

"I went out. Lady Kate's given us the day off." I crossed my arms over my chest. "I'd have told you but couldn't find you anywhere. Didn't you see my messages?"

Helen waved a hand in the air. "Nope. And I had a few Christmas bits to do. I wanted to get a head start, so I didn't get caught in the crowds. How exciting, though. A whole day off. What shall we do together?"

I was tempted to say I'd be reading alone, but I was burning with curiosity over what was going on with Zach. Surely, she'd say something about him visiting.

Helen's eyebrows rose when I didn't reply. "Is everything okay?"

"I'm figuring out what to do. I thought I'd be working."

"We do have a murder to solve. How about we grab breakfast and figure out our next move?"

"We could. I didn't know if you had other plans, though. Are you expecting visitors today?"

Helen's face was a picture of innocence. "Of course not. Who would visit me here?"

"You tell me."

"Um... You're being weird. Is your blood pressure low? Let's go to the kitchen. I'll make cranberry iced muffins, and we can have English breakfast tea. That'll improve your mood."

I wanted to tell her that wasn't the reason I was in a weird mood, but if Helen wasn't going to share her conversation with Zach and the reason for his visit, I wasn't dragging it out of her.

I was usually so good at putting the puzzle pieces together, but this mystery, not unlike Lord Albert's murder, had me stumped.

Once we were settled at the breakfast table, muffins in front of us and tea brewing in the pot, my thoughts turned back to Lord Albert, even though Helen's secretive behavior wasn't far behind.

"I've been thinking about the conversation you overheard," Helen said.

"Which one?" I mumbled around my muffin.

"How many conversations have you been secretly listening to?"

"You'd be surprised." I shrugged. "Go on."

"Lady Kate and her secret companion," Helen said. "Unless she's been speed dating, she can't already be in love. She only just lost her husband."

As if Helen had summoned Lord Albert by talking about him, he zoomed through the door in a whoosh of icy air.

Helen shivered. "Do we have company?"

I nodded. "Lord Albert, was your marriage to Lady Kate happy?"

His forehead wrinkled before he gave a firm nod of affirmation.

"Did you ever have concerns about her fidelity?"

His eyebrows rose, and he hovered closer before shaking his head.

"I overheard a conversation Lady Kate had on the phone. She told the other person she loved them and they'd be together soon. Who was she talking to?" I set my phone on the table, so he could use it if he wanted to do more than nod or shake his head.

Lord Albert simply shrugged.

"He doesn't think she cheated on him?" Helen said.

"It seems not."

"From what I've learned, they didn't spend much time together. Maybe Lord Albert overlooked signs of trouble. Gunner can be like that when I'm hinting I want something done around the house."

"What signs would they be?"

"Oh, you know, hushed conversations when no one else is around, sending text messages on the sly, and leaving the room when your phone rings. That's all dubious."

I bit the inside of my cheek. Helen was describing her own behavior. "Perhaps we should get Gunner to look into Lady Kate's phone records? The call she received will have been logged."

Helen's nose wrinkled. "He'll need authorization to do that. I could twist his arm, but I don't want to get him in trouble. My hubby can't be locked up over Christmas, especially since I expect him to dress as Santa on the big day when he carves the turkey."

"Of course not. We can't miss out on Gunner being Mr. Jolly."

Helen shot me a sharp look. "Or get arrested and lose his job."

"That, too." I looked back at Lord Albert. "I could only hear one side of the conversation. I may be getting things wrong."

His face registered his concern. He jabbed at my phone for a minute before showing me the screen.

"It's an online dating site." Helen peered at it. "Why's he showing you that?"

"You think Lady Kate was looking online for love?" I asked him.

Lord Albert shrugged again, although didn't seem eager to meet my gaze, which suggested he knew more than he was letting on.

"Why don't you see if you can find her on there?"

He looked horrified at the suggestion.

"It'll keep you busy and stop you from worrying about Julian," I said.

"It's how most people meet their partners these days," Helen said. "They fill in all those awkward, soul-searching questions and get given a perfect match. Although it never worked when I tried. People lie on those profiles. I once met a man who claimed he was six-foot five. He was the same height as me, and that was when I wasn't wearing heels."

The rumble of a large vehicle pulling up outside the front of the house had me hopping up. "We're not expecting any deliveries today, are we?"

Helen shook her head. "Not that I know of. Unless Annie's changed something on the schedule."

With a half-eaten muffin still in my hand and questions whirling around my head that needed answers, I headed to the front door and peered out. There was a lorry outside, and the driver was opening the back. He nodded when he saw me watching.

I hurriedly finished my muffin, brushed crumbs off my fingers, and went out to meet him. "What have you got in there?"

"Three marquees, a dozen jumbo-sized heating units, and a pile of tables and chairs. Where do you want them?"

I did a quick mental flick over the schedule for the Winter Wonderland Gala. "You're two days early."

"The boss said to deliver them today, or you wouldn't get them until after Christmas. The weather up north is set to close in, and we couldn't risk not being able to get in and out. These country places are beautiful, but try driving a lorry along the lanes after a snowstorm."

"Oh, I suppose so. We're not ready for you, though."

"How long will it take for you to get ready?"

Helen came out and joined me. "What's going on?"

"The outdoor equipment is here, and the backyard patio area is covered in snow. It'll need to be cleared before we put anything out."

"I guess it means you ladies need to get sweeping." The driver chuckled. "It'll take me a good hour to get everything unloaded, so you've got time."

Helen groaned. "So much for a day off."

"We could see if anyone else can help. The cleaning staff may still be around," I said.

"No, I saw them leave half an hour ago."

"Where were you half an hour ago? Here?" I said. "I looked for you everywhere."

"Oh, I was around and about. You must have missed me."

Or she'd been hiding. "Maybe there's someone in the kitchen who could lend a hand."

"You take a look. I'll go find some brooms."

I headed into the kitchen, and inconveniently, the place was empty. The kitchen staff were most likely hiding to avoid any extra work. I didn't blame them. Who wanted to shovel snow in freezing conditions?

While the driver was unloading the lorry, I dashed through to the back and found Helen waiting with two large brooms, so we set to work clearing the huge patio area.

A window opened above my head, and I looked up to see Annie peering out. "What are you up to?"

"We've had an early delivery. I need to get this space ready for the marquees."

"Did they call ahead to say they were arriving early?"

"If they did, I missed it." I frantically swept away snow. "I thought maybe they'd contacted you."

She shook her head. "They have my mobile number, but they may have called the office. I haven't been down to check any calls. What a mess. I wish I could help."

"You rest your foot. We'll get it ready."

"Thanks. I'd have been frantic if they'd shown up and it was just me and my messed up foot. I'm going to call the company and tell them I'm not happy."

"The driver said it was because of the bad weather. At least we've got all the indoor equipment for the gala. It would have been worse if they got snowed in and missed our delivery."

"Oh, I suppose so. Good for you, looking at the positive. I'll be down soon." Annie pulled her head in and slid the window shut.

I kept sweeping, staying on the opposite side of the patio to Helen. I looked over at her a few times, but her head was down as she worked, not seeming to have a care in the world.

"This is good exercise," she finally said.

"Sure." I kept sweeping.

"It'll help keep off those extra Christmas pounds. I always gain half a stone, thanks to all the delicious treats I bake."

"It will."

Helen stopped sweeping and looked at me. "Is everything okay?"

I hated secrets, and I wanted the truth to come out. Maybe I was making too much of this. Whatever Zach and Helen were having secret meetings about, it might be nothing to do with me.

I propped the broom against the wall. "Helen, what were you doing talking to Zach this morning?"

She froze and then jerked upright. "How do you know about that?"

"I heard you outside. I'd been out with Julian—"

"Wait a second, you went off with Julian?"

"I was going to tell you, but I got distracted when I discovered you talking to Zach. What was he doing here? Had you been with him all morning? Why didn't he want to see me?"

Helen set aside her broom and walked over. "I will answer your questions, but answer mine first. You were with Julian on your own? After everything that happened in the cemetery?"

"If you bothered to check your phone messages, I told you what I was doing. And I had Flipper with me. I was safe."

"The battery died, and I forgot to charge it overnight, so I left it in my room." Helen pursed her lips. "You should have taken me with you."

"I would have, but you were meeting Zach."

"Yes! Well, there's a good reason for that." Helen smoothed a hand down her curls. "Lorna, be careful around Julian. He could be dangerous."

"I don't think he is. Julian gets confused when he doesn't take his medication, but he's not a threat. He jumped out a window to get away from his mom, and I saw him do it. And you're right, we need to help him. He's struggling with the ghosts. So I took him somewhere quiet, and we talked. He's terrified by what he sees and doesn't think anyone understands him."

"Still, that was a risky move."

"I had to do it alone. You were missing." I arched an eyebrow, waiting for Helen to explain herself.

"Did your conversation help Julian?"

My eyes narrowed at her continued avoidance. "I think so. The more I talk to him, the more I believe he didn't kill Lord Albert."

"But Julian confessed in the mausoleum," Helen said.

"While under extreme stress and off medication that keeps his mental state stable. I think, if we help him figure out how to handle the ghosts, he won't need all that medication."

"Okay. But you know Zach won't be happy if he learns what you've been up to."

"He can't lecture me, since he's also keeping secrets with you. Tell me what's going on."

Helen looked around before returning her gaze to me. "I didn't want to say anything until I was certain."

"Certain about what?"

She grinned. "I'm expecting a new arrival. Our family is about to get bigger."

I engulfed her in a hug. "You're pregnant! That's amazing. Why didn't you say something sooner?"

Helen squirmed in my grip, laughing as she did so. "No, not a baby. I'm expecting a puppy. After we went to the animal shelter with Mary, I couldn't stop thinking about a scruffy ginger pup I'd seen on his own. That little guy burrowed into my heart. So, I contacted the animal shelter to see if he was still available. I figured someone must have picked him after that event, but he was still there."

"A puppy, not a baby?" I stepped back. "This has all been about you getting another dog?"

"Yep. What else would it be? I'm a puppy fur mother. Well, almost."

"I'm happy for you and the pup, but are you sure about taking on a puppy? I love them, but they're almost as hard work as a newborn."

"Absolutely. And I know what people say about puppies. They're basically babies with teeth and you can't put a nappy on them, but I'm in love. And I'm sure he'll be accepted into the household. Milly has met him, and I know Flipper will take care of him."

"Of course, Flipper loves all animals. But what does this puppy have to do with Zach visiting you in secret?"

"It wasn't exactly a secret, but he couldn't stop for long. And I can't have the puppy here. So I asked Zach to help by taking the pup."

"Why not Gunner?"

"Because the puppy is one of his Christmas gifts." Helen laughed. "At least, that's what I'm telling him. That pup is all mine. I can't let him see his gift before the big day, though. So Zach is keeping him safe until Christmas Day."

I groaned and tipped my head back. "You shouldn't have kept this from me. I was thinking the worst."

"You were? You don't trust me with Zach?"

"Of course, I do." My cheeks heated. Maybe I'd had a second of doubt. "But you kept having those strange conversations you wouldn't tell me about. And then I found Zach here with you. My brain was working on overdrive."

"Lorna! Sometimes, you have too much imagination for your own good."

"I'm sorry. I should have known better."

"You should, but you're forgiven. And I hope you don't mind there being a new addition to the family. I thought it would be a fun surprise."

"Not for a second." I hugged her again. "But please, no more surprises."

"I make no promises."

I jerked as something cold slammed into my back.

"What is it?" Helen pulled away from me as I staggered forward.

I turned to find Lord Albert in my face, pointing at the phone in my pocket. "I think Lord Albert's found something. It seems important." I pulled out my phone and held it for him to use.

After several painful minutes and lots of spelling mistakes, I finally made sense of Lord Albert's message. The words made my heart pound. *Kate dating profile real.*

"What is it?" Helen stared at the screen.

"Lord Albert's found Lady Kate's secret. She's been looking for love behind his back."

# Chapter 19

"How should we handle this?" Helen stood behind me as we studied the dating profile Lord Albert had found on his wife.

"I'm not sure, but we need to confront Lady Kate. She must have found a new guy and wanted to get rid of her husband. It's a great motive for murder."

Lord Albert swirled around the room, making his displeasure clear at this news.

"The profile's not old." Helen was studying the information. "She set it up a few months before Lord Albert died."

"She must have gotten lucky quickly," I said. "Lady Kate found a match and realized she no longer wanted to be married to Lord Albert."

"So why not ask for a divorce? Killing him is extreme."

"I'm assuming Lady Kate inherited everything when he died. Not only did she get a new guy, but she also amassed a heap of assets," I said.

"It says on her profile she's looking for her one true love and needs someone who will keep up with her passion. Maybe Lord Albert wasn't able to perform in the bedroom." Helen grimaced. "How awkward."

I looked at Lord Albert, but he had his back to us. "Are you going to bring up the subject with him?"

"No! But we need to find a way to ask Lady Kate about this," Helen said.

"What do you need to ask me?" Lady Kate walked into the office, a smile on her face. It faded the second she saw our serious expressions. "Is something wrong? Is it Julian?"

It was time to take the reindeer by the antlers and deal with this matter. I turned the computer screen so Lady Kate could see it.

She blinked several times and swallowed. "What are you doing looking at that?"

"Trying to find out what really happened to Lord Albert," I said. "Ever since we arrived, we've heard worrying rumors about his death."

"I expect most of those rumors came from his killer, Emma." Lady Kate glared at the computer screen.

"Some did. But other people are worried, too. They want to know the truth. Were you and Lord Albert having problems before he died?"

Lady Kate sank into a chair and massaged her forehead with her fingertips. "Since you've seen that, there's no use saying my marriage was perfect. I cared for Albert, but we were more friends than anything else. I thought I'd be happy with a kind, generous man. And it was enough to begin with. But over the years, there was something lacking."

"You mean, no passion?" Helen said.

Lady Kate's cheeks flushed. "Yes. And I missed it. We would cuddle and hold hands, but he didn't want anything else. Not long after I had Julian, Albert said he didn't see me in the same way."

"That's a long time to live in a loveless marriage," I said.

"There was affection, but I'd gotten frustrated about his lack of interest. I'm an attractive woman, and I have a lot to offer a man. I didn't want to let any more years go by and miss out on being adored in every way. I talked to Albert about it several times, but he said we had enough. We had our children, a beautiful home, successful careers, and a great social life."

"It wasn't enough for you?" I said.

"I tried to be happy, and sometimes, I was. But there were other times when I'd find myself in a crowded room, surrounded by friends and family, Albert by my side, and I felt so lonely I wanted to weep. I'd have given all this up to have a man love me in the way I deserve."

Lord Albert floated over slowly. I'd expected to see anger on his face, but he looked devastated. His shoulders were slumped, and he was shaking his head as he swiped at his eyes.

"You met someone through this online dating site?" I said.

"That profile should have been removed. No one should be able to see that. How did you find it?"

"We got lucky," Helen said. "Once something is on the internet, it's almost impossible to get rid of it."

Lady Kate's eyes narrowed a fraction. "I used an exclusive, discrete agency. They assured me no one would find out about this. I certainly paid them enough to make sure this was never discovered."

"Then you should ask for a refund. Did they help you find someone?" I said.

"A match was made, and I met him. We took it slowly, talking on the phone to begin with. Then we met once a week. I swiftly realized he was what I wanted." She pressed a hand against her forehead and closed her eyes. "I'm mortified. I wish I'd told Albert what I'd planned while he was alive. But how do you discuss this with your husband? I'd have appeared ungrateful. And he gave me so much."

"Lord Albert didn't give you enough of what you really needed," I said. "It's understandable why you looked elsewhere."

"Perhaps." Lady Kate pushed the screen away. "I hope we can keep this between us. I don't want Celeste and Julian to find out. They'd hate me."

"I'm not sure we can. You see, I don't think your husband's death was an accident. Having discovered this information, it gives you an excellent motive for murdering him."

Her mouth opened before she snapped her jaw shut. "It was the cook's incompetence. Emma gave him nuts when she knew he wasn't supposed to eat them. Everyone knows that."

"Do they? Emma's protesting her innocence, and the police didn't find anything against her."

She huffed out a breath. "Why are you so interested in what happened to my late husband?"

"Because this unfinished business is tearing your family apart. Julian almost confessed to his dad's murder because he's so confused. Wouldn't you like a resolution to this? You must want to know what happened, so you can clear Julian's name."

"And Emma's name, too," Helen said.

"I'm not so sure she is innocent," Lady Kate muttered. She let out a long sigh. "But I would like this to be over. It's been hanging over our heads ever since Albert died. I... I was convinced Emma was involved."

"You're not so sure anymore?" I said.

"I'm not sure about much these days." Lady Kate stared out the window, although I wasn't certain she was looking at anything. "Emma was excellent in the kitchen. She didn't make mistakes. And I miss her food."

"And there's no proof she did it," I said.

Lady Kate stiffened. "She could have done it. Emma did the last-minute checks to make sure everything was up to standard. She shouldn't have let this happen. Albert would still be alive if it wasn't for her."

"What was her motive, though?"

"I... I don't know. Emma always seemed happy here. And we paid her well. I can't think of one. That doesn't mean she's innocent."

"If Emma didn't do it, someone else must have put nuts into Lord Albert's dinner," I said.

"Not me. And not Julian," Lady Kate said. "I know he confessed, but he was frightened. He doesn't always know what he's saying. It's the pills he's on."

"I agree with you. I don't think Julian did it either," I said.

"You do? You think he's innocent?"

"I think so." The hopeful look in Lady Kate's eyes had me softening toward her. She was far from perfect, but she loved her son. And if she had killed her husband, surely, she wouldn't let Julian be charged with the crime.

"I keep wondering whether this was all a horrible mix-up," Lady Kate said. "Someone in the kitchen simply put the wrong ingredients in the meal. People make mistakes all the time. I know I do. I did with my marriage to Albert."

"I don't disagree with you, but I believe only Lord Albert had nuts in his dinner that night, didn't he?"

She leveled me with a cool stare. "You are well informed. Yes, all our food was checked, and it was only his plate that had the nuts."

"Which means it was a deliberate act. Someone knew about your husband's allergy and used it to their advantage."

"But who? I know I didn't do it, Julian didn't do it, and it couldn't have been Celeste. Annie could barely walk, and Emma swears her innocence. And, as you rightly pointed out, she has no motive. Why would someone want Albert dead?"

"They wanted him dead so they could move on with their new relationship," Helen said.

"You still think it was me." Lady Kate's voice was flat. She was quiet for a moment. "I see how you might. After all, I had been cheating. Well, we didn't do anything until after Albert died. Only sent flirty text messages to each other. Oh, dear. I've been such an idiot."

"Were you planning on finishing things with Lord Albert?" I said. "Since you found this other guy, you must have been considering a divorce."

"I was wondering about it, but didn't want to distress the children. Celeste had already gone through one divorce when Albert left Mary, and Julian has always been fragile. I was scared what a divorce would do to him. You've seen how vulnerable he is."

"You were planning on staying in the marriage and carrying on an affair?" I said.

"I doubt Albert would have noticed what I did. He was so busy with his charity work. Sometimes, I didn't see him for days. And I was lonely. I didn't realize how much I needed a companion until I met one. Someone who could offer me everything and not just parts of a relationship." Lady Kate looked away, her hands clenched. "I hadn't decided what I was going to do, but I knew things needed to change."

Which again gave Lady Kate an excellent motive for killing her husband. I looked at Lord Albert to gauge his feelings on the revelation about Lady Kate's affair. He still looked sad, his eyes down as he drifted around. It must be a shock to learn he'd been living a lie. But maybe he knew things weren't right and had simply not addressed them. Lady Kate had been in the same situation for a long time until she'd taken action. And unfortunately, that action made her the prime suspect in Lord Albert's murder.

"Will you tell the police about this?" Lady Kate said.

I looked at Helen, and she gave a small shrug. "Not yet. After all, it doesn't prove anything, other than you were in an unhappy marriage."

"It wasn't unhappy. It just wasn't full of the love I craved. I wish things could have been different. But I didn't kill my husband."

A thud outside and the sound of tinkling bells had me looking out the window. I couldn't believe what I was seeing, so I hurried closer to get a better look. "It's a sleigh!"

Helen joined me at the window. "And six reindeer. Has Santa come early?"

"That's not supposed to be here for two days." Lady Kate joined us. "It's part of the gala party fun."

"Of course. The sleigh rides for guests." I watched as the sleigh owner hopped out and checked the reindeer. "I think I know what's going on. A driver showed up a short while ago with the outdoor marquees and heaters. Bad weather is setting in across parts of the country, so they're delivering early. It must be the same with the reindeer."

"I can't deal with this," Lady Kate said. "What am I supposed to do with six reindeer?"

"We'll deal with them," I said.

"I'm still not certain there should even be a party."

"If you want the party to happen, we'll ensure it does. And if you don't, we'll fix that, too," I said. "The party doesn't have to go ahead."

"But we keep the reindeer for a few days," Helen whispered in my ear. "They're so cute. And I want a sleigh ride in the snow."

Lady Kate pulled back her shoulders. "We're having the gala. I won't be defeated in my own home."

"Whatever you think best." I sensed the challenge in her voice. Lady Kate was a fighter.

She caught hold of my arm. "Lorna, Helen, I'd appreciate your discretion over the matter of my dating someone else. I know it doesn't look good, but I cared for Albert. I'd never hurt him. He was in such distress as he struggled to take his final breath. It was a cruel thing to do to him and an awful thing for Celeste and Julian to experience. I don't expect you to believe me, since you discovered the online profile, but I didn't do it."

Lady Kate sounded genuine, but so did all the suspects.

I gave her arm a quick pat and stepped away. "If you were guilty, you'd have fired me and Helen on the spot for poking around in your private business and exposing your secret."

"Hmmm, I suppose I should have." She smiled and shook her head. "But I won't do that. Annie has spoken highly about you since you arrived, and I trust her. Plus, I can't afford to let you go. The Winter Wonderland Gala will fall apart if you're not here. And if you're looking into what happened to my husband and perhaps even able to uncover the truth, I can hardly complain. I know that truth won't lead you to me, so I have nothing to worry about."

Even though Lady Kate was top of the suspect list, I was having doubts about her guilt. "I appreciate your confidence in us."

"If you think you can do the job the police can't, then carry on. But please don't gossip about this dating secret with other people. This is my life and my child's life, after all."

"We won't gossip," Helen said. "We really do want to help lay a ghost to rest, though."

Lord Albert nodded at her.

I looked out the window as two reindeer pranced past. Although there was still a murder to solve, first, we needed to deal with some feisty four-legged arrivals and a huge sleigh.

# Chapter 20

I was almost not surprised to find Helen missing the next morning when I got up. It was becoming her routine, sneaking out and making plans without telling me. I tried not to mind. After all, she was keeping her Christmas puppy a secret, but I didn't like not being included. We always used to do everything together. Things felt like they were changing, and not for the better, as far as I was concerned.

"Well, Flipper, it's just you and me." I petted his soft fur, always loving how being with my best fluffy buddy calmed me down and got rid of any glum mood.

Lord Albert drifted into my bedroom as I climbed out of bed.

"Oh, and a ghost, too." I smiled at Lord Albert.

He raised his hand in acknowledgement and drifted to the window.

"How are you feeling after finding out about Lady Kate's affair?" I shrugged into my pink dressing gown and padded to the window to join him. I set my phone on the ledge so he could use it, but he didn't touch the phone and simply shrugged. "You knew things weren't right between you, didn't you?"

He nodded.

"Was it bad enough that Lady Kate would kill you?"

That earned me a vehement shake of his head.

"Since you're here, we may as well go over the suspects. I had Lady Kate at the top of the list, but after talking to her yesterday, I'm not so sure."

Lord Albert spent a minute puzzling over my phone before *not her* appeared.

"You don't think it was anyone, though. Unless you gave those nuts to yourself... You didn't, did you?"

He pursed his lips and raised his eyebrows.

"Fair enough. But I had to ask. Let's start with Emma, your cook. I discounted her. Sure, she had easy access to your meal, so she could have put the nuts in it, but there's no reason for her to want you dead. From what Lady Kate said, she was paid well and enjoyed her work. And when we met Emma, she confirmed that. She was sad about your death. She even liked being around the rest of the family. Emma lost everything and gained nothing but a bad reputation and the risk of becoming homeless."

He nodded and pointed to the message he'd already typed on the phone.

"Emma's off the table. So is Annie. She can't walk and has no motive for wanting you gone. Much like Emma, her position could be vulnerable if Lady Kate makes changes."

He nodded again.

"So we move on to Mary. We caught her stealing from Lady Kate, but it's for an excellent cause. Not that I'm saying stealing is right, though. Did Mary ever hint that she regretted your divorce?"

Lord Albert shook his head.

"What about this unusual living situation? Maybe she was tiring of it. She wanted out but didn't feel she could leave in case it upset Celeste."

Lord Albert stumbled over the keypad a few times before getting out the message: *not trapped*.

"Mary still seems fond of you, but unless she's hiding some deep unhappiness, she doesn't have a great motive. And she wasn't at the dining table when you had your allergic reaction. I don't think it was Mary."

He typed out the word *agree*.

"And then we come to Lady Kate. Her motive is the strongest. She'd met another man and wanted to move on. She wasn't happy in a passionless marriage and needed more. Would you have let her go if she asked for a divorce?"

Lord Albert looked out the window for a minute before turning to me and nodding.

"Did you love her?"

He nodded again, then bent over the phone and typed out *as a friend*.

"And she must have realized that. Perhaps Lady Kate panicked. She thought you wouldn't let her go, or she'd lose her home if you divorced. Or did she get greedy and decide to take everything?"

He shook his head again.

"I'm still not certain about her. Lady Kate would have had the opportunity to put nuts in your food during dinner. She sat beside you. I have to keep her on the list."

His scowl told me what he thought about that, but I couldn't let go of a suspect who had such a great motive. And more than one motive.

"Let's move on to your children."

Lord Albert waved his hands in the air.

"I know. It must be hard to consider that one of them hurt you. But Julian is troubled. Perhaps he made a terrible mistake. Were you in any fights before you died? Was there a reason for him to be angry with you?"

Lord Albert typed NOTHING on the phone in capital letters.

"He told me his medication had horrible side effects. He thought you looked unnatural and evil. It must have been a hallucination. Maybe that was enough for him to try something rash. He may not even have been aware he was doing it."

Lord Albert typed the word *accident*.

"Possibly. He didn't intend to kill you. He was struggling, and unfortunately, you became a part of his delusions. Julian needs to stay on the suspect list. But if it's any comfort, if he hurt you, I don't think he meant it. And I've offered to help him get used to seeing ghosts. It can be frightening. When I first started seeing them, there were times when I didn't know what was real. I'm not sure if I'll be able to do much for Julian, but it could help."

Lord Albert pressed his hands together in a prayer position and mouthed the word *thank you*.

"That leaves us with Celeste. And she confuses me. When I first met her, Celeste seemed sweet and determined to help you. And she's convinced you were killed. Is that because she knows what really happened?"

Lord Albert bent over the phone. He took several minutes to type out *childish, no killer*.

"It's more than that. Celeste has a mean streak. We shouldn't overlook her. And she has a temper, too. She hit you. Was she holding a grudge against you? She wanted revenge and things got out of hand. Perhaps she only meant to scare you and didn't realize how serious it would get so quickly."

He crossed his arms over his chest and glared at me.

"And Celeste was in the dining room. She sits right by you, too. Do you remember her causing a distraction or making you look away from your food? It would have been all she needed to take the risk and add those nuts."

He considered my question before shaking his head.

"Well, we still have three suspects. Lady Kate, Julian, and Celeste. Until I find some evidence or someone slips up and says something they shouldn't, I'm stuck. I'm not sure I can help you, Lord Albert."

His gaze turned sorrowful, and he moved slowly around my bedroom.

"If you have to stay here as a ghost, it won't be so bad. You'll see your family every day, and you can watch your children flourish. Although you may also need to watch Lady Kate with her new man. I'm not sure how you'd feel about that."

He shrugged and continued to drift around, looking as confused as I felt.

My phone rang, and I lifted it, not recognizing the number. "Hello, Lorna Shadow."

"Hey, Miss Shadow. Annie gave me your number. There's been a problem with delivering the festive floral arrangements for your party."

"A problem? We were expecting you around lunchtime tomorrow. Will you be late?"

"I won't be there at all. My truck is stuck over two hundred miles away."

My gaze went to the window. Although there had been snowfall overnight, there were only a couple of fresh inches on the ground. "Is there any way you can get here?"

"I'll try, but I'm promising nothing. You should look into making alternative arrangements or do without the flowers."

Without flowers, the marquees would look bare. "Do what you can to get here. I'll figure out a backup plan."

"Good luck with that. And Happy Christmas!"

I ended the call with my own muted seasons greetings. "Lord Albert, I have to get to work. We have a flower emergency. I promise, the second I get a chance, we'll go through all the evidence again. I'd love to give you closure, but we might need a Christmas miracle to make it happen."

He nodded before fading away.

I dressed quickly and dashed downstairs to speak to Annie. She wasn't in the office, and after a quick check in the kitchen, the staff confirmed they hadn't seen her.

After fixing Flipper his breakfast and leaving him in the kitchen, I headed back upstairs and knocked on Annie's bedroom door. She didn't answer.

"Are you awake? Sorry to bother you. It's Lorna. We have a problem with the flowers."

There was no reply.

I pushed the door open a few inches and peered inside. The curtains were open and the bed made. "Annie, I need to speak to you."

The place was empty. I stepped inside and eased the door shut. She must have been up and out early for me to miss her.

I checked the attached bathroom, but it was also empty. I was about to leave the bathroom when I noticed men's cologne by the sink. There was also a man's tie wrapped around the door handle.

Annie mentioned having a boyfriend, but I didn't know he stayed here. I sniffed the cologne. The bottle looked expensive and smelled of woody, sweet musk.

I walked out of the bathroom and slowed. Poking out from under the bed looked to be a foot cast. Exactly like the one Annie wore. I glanced at the closed bedroom door then went to the side of the bed and ducked down. I pulled out the cast and inspected it. Maybe this was a spare. But surely, she shouldn't take the cast off her foot while she was healing. Was that even possible?

As I turned the cast over, there was writing on the bottom. *Hoping for a speedy recovery. Best wishes, Albert.* There was also a single kiss.

That was the only signature on it.

I eased the cast back under the bed but met resistance. I peered underneath it and discovered a shoebox in the way. I pulled it out and opened the lid. Inside was a gorgeous pair of sky-high, bright red heels. The receipt was in the box, and they'd only been bought two weeks ago.

They must be a gift for someone. Annie wouldn't be wearing heels anytime soon. Even if she didn't have to have surgery on her foot, she'd have months of physical therapy ahead of her and would always have to be careful with her ankle. Wearing terrifying heels like this would be the last thing she'd be thinking about.

As I eased everything back under the bed, I noticed another small box. Feeling more than a little guilty about poking around in Annie's things, I pulled it out. It was a box full of letters. A quick shift through them revealed they were love notes she'd written, most likely to her boyfriend.

I tucked them away. I wasn't here to poke around in Annie's private life.

I sat back on my heels and did a slow visual inspection of the room. I'd never questioned Annie's injury, but finding that cast and the shoes had me doubting her. Why would she fake her injury, though?

My gaze settled on a vase of stunning white roses. I stood, walked over, and sniffed one.

Rapid footsteps approached the room, making me freeze. Maybe it was a maid coming to turn down the bed or vacuum. I headed to the door and opened it to discover Annie on the other side, her hand reaching for the doorknob.

She blinked at me and took a step back. "Lorna! What are you doing in here?"

"Um... Looking for you. There's been a problem with a delivery." I looked at her foot. She still wore a cast, but if that had been her walking toward the room, she'd been going fast, even with her crutches.

Annie's forehead furrowed as she glanced over my shoulder. "Oh! Well, I'll be down soon to help with that. You shouldn't be in here."

"Sorry, but Helen's not around, and I needed to run some ideas past you."

"Very well. Give me five minutes." Annie moved past me, her steps much slower.

"Did you have an early morning appointment?" I stayed by the door, my gaze on her foot. The spare cast, the high heels, and the change in pace the second Annie realized she wasn't alone. This was adding up to something worrying.

"Go downstairs. I'll join you when I'm ready."

She'd never been this brusque with me before. I didn't move. "How's your foot?"

"Sore! I've been on it too much already, today." Annie shot me an irritated look. "I just need a few minutes on my own. So, if you don't mind..."

I couldn't leave this alone and had to find out if Annie was faking her injury.

Lord Albert floated through the door as I was figuring out what to say to her. I was glad he'd arrived. I'd need a witness if this went the way I thought it would.

"Were you at a doctor's appointment for your injured foot?" I said.

Annie rounded on me. "Why the sudden interest in my foot?"

"Oh, no reason. I love those white roses. Were they a gift from your boyfriend?"

"Yes, if you must know. He's always doing sweet things like that. He's a gentleman." Annie's gaze moved pointedly to the corridor.

"It's funny, but when I saw Lord Albert's grave, there was a single white rose on top of it."

Annie's eyes narrowed. "Why is that funny?"

"Maybe not funny, more coincidental. Your boyfriend sends you white roses identical to the one left on Lord Albert's headstone."

"Life is full of coincidences." Annie gestured at the door.

"I expect you'll be glad to get that cast off. And you must be sick of having to wear such sensible shoes all the time."

Her lips pursed. "Of course."

"You can get back to dancing around in high heels."

Annie's gaze cut to her bed. She noticed the cast poking out and dashed over and kicked it out of sight.

"What's going on?" I said.

"Other than you poking around in business that doesn't concern you, nothing." Annie remained by the bed, as if guarding it.

"That's not true," I said. "Did you really hurt your ankle?"

"Yes! Why would I make that up?"

"To make sure no one thought you killed Lord Albert."

# Chapter 21

A choked sounding laugh came out of Annie. She stalked to the door, no longer limping, and slammed it shut. "Don't say things like that. This place runs on rumors. I'll be fired as quickly as Emma if you breathe a word of that lie to anyone. I'm not losing my job because you're a nosy gossip. Why were you really poking around in my room? And don't lie and say it's because of a problem with a delivery."

Annie was blocking the only exit, so I stood my ground. "The festive floral arrangements are stuck because of the snow. Helen has gone out already, so I hoped you might help me come up with some solutions. When I got here, I discovered your bedroom empty—"

"And couldn't resist nosing around. That's all you've done since you got here, asked questions about things that have nothing to do with you. You're lucky Lady Kate hasn't slung you out for poking about in private family matters."

"Why would she? Helen and I are excellent at our jobs. You even told her that yourself."

"Excellent at faking it, more like. I didn't trust you the second I met you," Annie said. "I'm telling Lady

Kate about this. You've probably looked around her bedroom, too. She'll fire you. I've been loyal to her for years, so she'll believe anything I tell her."

"Don't you mean, you were loyal to Lord Albert for years? After all, you were in love with him, weren't you?"

Annie glared at me. "I have a boyfriend. You know that. We've talked about him."

"You have a fantasy about having a boyfriend. How long did you love Lord Albert?"

Her face turned red then pale. "You don't know what you're saying. Lord Albert was my employer."

I looked at Lord Albert as he hovered close by Annie, staring at her with astonishment on his face. "He was, but he was much more than that to you. Did he know how you felt about him?"

"Be quiet! You'll get us in trouble. I won't keep silent about this intrusion into my room."

"My snooping will be meaningless when people find out you killed Lord Albert. How will Lady Kate react to that?"

Annie shrieked and lunged at me. Her cast-covered foot slowed her just enough for me to dodge out of the way as she swung a clumsy punch at my face.

"Annie, it's over. You put the nuts in Lord Albert's food, didn't you?"

She gave another shriek and tried to grab me. "You're ruining everything. Life was good before you showed up. Leave me alone."

"It can't have been that good. You murdered the man you loved."

"This way. I heard a scream." That was Celeste's voice in the corridor.

"No! I don't want anyone else to know about this." Annie ran to the door and tried to hold it closed, but it was shoved open from the other side.

Celeste burst through, with Julian beside her. "What's happening? Kate heard a cry of distress, so we came to take a look."

"It was nothing. A misunderstanding." Annie's face was flushed again and damp with sweat. "I'm talking about the gala with Lorna."

"Is something the matter?" Lady Kate appeared by the door, closely followed by Mary.

"No, Lady Kate. Lorna was worried because there's a problem with a delivery. We'll sort it out." Annie's gaze was frantic as she looked at me, an expression of desperation on her face.

I shook my head. She couldn't think I'd cover for her after everything I'd discovered in her room.

"Annie, is something wrong? You don't look well," Lady Kate said. "Is your foot troubling you?"

"It's not troubling her," I said, "because she faked her injury. Annie can walk just fine."

No one spoke for several seconds, all eyes on the cast and boot strapped around Annie's foot.

"That's not possible. I was there when she fell off the ladder," Lady Kate said.

"Did you see her fall?" I said.

She paused. "I heard the thump as she landed, and then Annie cried out in pain."

"And did you inspect the ankle injury?"

"Of course not. I'm not a doctor."

"What about the paramedics who took her away?"

"Oh, well, Annie has a friend in the area who's a doctor." Lady Kate sucked in a breath. "He collected her. Annie said she didn't want any fuss, and emergency transport wasn't needed. I tried to convince her otherwise, but her doctor friend arrived quickly, checked the ankle, and took her off in his car."

"I didn't need to go to the hospital to have my ankle fixed," Annie said. "It wasn't necessary. And I'd rather be treated by my friend than prodded around by a strange doctor just coming off a double shift."

"May I speak to your doctor friend?" I said.

"No! Why bother him?"

Annie wouldn't let me speak to him because he wasn't a real doctor, I was sure of it. Maybe it was someone she'd paid to act the role or a friend thinking it was a joke to pretend to be a doctor. "Tell us why you have more than one plaster cast for your foot. Surely, you wouldn't be able to take that off. Unless the casts aren't real."

Annie's sigh showed her annoyance. "I can't take it off. And I use this boot to give it an extra layer of protection. I am injured!"

"I suspect you're using the boot to make sure the cast doesn't come off on its own," I said.

"Lorna, this is all confusing. Why would Annie fake her ankle injury?" Mary said.

I looked at Lord Albert, who still appeared stunned by the revelations. "Because her injury eliminated her from being Lord Albert's killer. If she could barely walk, she wouldn't be able to sneak into the kitchen, doctor his food, and not be seen."

"But why would Annie want Lord Albert dead?" Mary asked. "They got along well."

"Because Annie was in love with him," I said. "And that love wasn't returned. It must have driven her mad to care about someone so deeply and not be with him in the way she wanted. I expect you understand that, Lady Kate. Probably you, too, Mary. Your relationships with Lord Albert weren't what you wanted. That must have been frustrating."

"Annie has a boyfriend," Lady Kate said. "She often talks about him. She didn't love my husband."

"Have you ever met this boyfriend?" I said.

"Well, no. But he works away, I believe."

"He can't be away that much, since his cologne and tie are in Annie's bathroom."

Annie lunged at the bathroom door and stood in front of it. "Don't go in there. It's not clean."

"Your boyfriend has never stayed here," Lady Kate said. "At least, you've never informed me you were having a guest to stay."

"I thought you wouldn't allow it, so I snuck him in." Annie kept guarding the bathroom door, her hands in fists by her sides.

Celeste and Julian were watching her with wide eyes.

"What are you hiding in there?" Julian said.

"Nothing! I just don't like my private things looked at." She jabbed a finger at me. "And that's exactly what Lorna's been doing. Lady Kate, you can't trust her. You must fire her. If she's been snooping around my bedroom, she'll have been looking through your personal effects as well."

Lady Kate regarded me shrewdly. "I'm well aware of Miss Shadow's investigative habits. She's uncovered many secrets, including yours, Annie. Now, move aside. We need to see inside your bathroom."

"What's in there has nothing to do with Lorna's baseless accusations about me and Lord Albert." Annie splayed her arms wide. "I respected him. And I love my job. I'd do nothing to jeopardize my position here."

"Move aside, now," Lady Kate commanded.

With a sigh, Annie stepped away, her angry glare fixed on me.

Lady Kate and Mary marched into the bathroom and looked around, keeping the door open so we could all see what they discovered.

"This is Albert's tie." Mary stroked the red and green tie wrapped around the door handle. "I bought it for him as a birthday present."

"And this is his cologne." Lady Kate held up the bottle I'd discovered by the sink. "Annie, what are you doing with my husband's things in your bathroom?"

Annie stammered out a few words, her gaze going to Celeste. "It wasn't me."

"Were you having an affair with Albert?" Lady Kate strode back into the bedroom, Mary by her side, the women united in their quest to find their husband's killer.

Lord Albert drifted beside me. He was shaking his head as he pointed at Annie.

"From what I've gathered, the love was one-sided," I said. "Annie had a crush on Lord Albert, but he was always faithful. You'll find love letters Annie wrote to Lord Albert under her bed. She never received any in return."

He nodded several times and pointed to the wedding band on his finger.

"Albert took matrimony seriously," Mary said. "We discussed separating for months before he decided to leave me. It took him a long time to come to terms with our failed marriage. He wouldn't ruin his marriage to Kate for an affair."

Lady Kate was by the bed, pulling things out from beneath it. She removed the extra cast, the box with the high heels, and the love notes, which she pawed over.

"That isn't proof." Annie's face grew scarlet as she watched Lady Kate. "There are no names in those letters. They're for my boyfriend, so you shouldn't read them."

"Why haven't you sent them to him?" Lady Kate said. "You've hidden them under your bed like a child with a naughty secret. I need to speak to your boyfriend. That's if he's real."

"No! He has nothing to do with this."

"I have one more question," I said. "When any of you visit Lord Albert's grave, do you ever notice a white rose on the headstone?"

Lady Kate paused from her study of the love letters. "There's a new one there every week. There has been since he died. As soon as he was buried, a rose appeared on the soil. Then, when we had the headstone fitted, one showed up there. I asked the children and Mary about it, but none of them knew who left it. I assumed it was a friend from the village who stopped by. Why do you ask?"

My gaze went to the vase of white roses on Annie's cabinet. "Because Annie has been visiting Lord Albert's final resting place. She leaves a symbol of her undying love each time she does."

Annie was almost crimson with rage. Her hands were clenched by her sides and her top lip pulled back. "You can't prove any of this. Lorna is lying. Get rid of her."

"We can prove you don't have a boyfriend, and we can prove you faked your ankle injury," I said.

"And those items in your bathroom belonged to Albert," Mary said. "It makes no sense they would be in there, unless you took them."

"And what about these love notes to Albert?" Lady Kate said. "You really killed him?"

"It wasn't me." Annie's gaze went back to Julian and Celeste. "I didn't put the nuts in his food."

I looked at Julian. He was pale and shaking, and his gaze kept darting to his dad. Celeste simply looked angry.

"Annie, if you loved Lord Albert as much as you claim you do, you must realize what a precarious situation Julian is in. He's confused and thinks he killed his father," I said. "Would you let a child of the man you adored go down for this crime? A crime you committed."

Annie closed her eyes and let out a slow sigh. "Julian had nothing to do with this. He's innocent."

"Is that a confession?" Lady Kate said.

Annie opened her eyes and looked at Celeste. "I promise you all I didn't kill Lord Albert. I loved him dearly, but that love wasn't returned."

I looked at Celeste. She was chewing on her bottom lip, and her eyes were narrowed. "Annie, you didn't do this alone, did you?"

Annie moistened her lips with her tongue. "I made the biggest mistake of my life. I confided in someone I considered a friend. Everything went wrong after that."

My gaze settled on Celeste, and I arched an eyebrow. "Celeste?"

"No!" Mary said. "My daughter isn't involved in this."

A cold smirk crossed Annie's face. "Celeste is up to her neck in lies. She's worse than me. Her spite made her kill her own father."

"Shut up! We're not real friends," Celeste yelled.

Annie looked away, but the coldness remained in her eyes as she ducked her head. "I didn't want Lord Albert dead, but I wanted to teach him a lesson after he rejected me."

I nodded slowly as the pieces clicked into place. "You got someone who cared for you involved in a game, didn't you? Did you suggest it would be fun to give Lord Albert just a few nuts? You told your accomplice they wouldn't hurt him and he was exaggerating about how bad his allergy was?"

Annie's head remained lowered. "I never meant for Celeste to take me seriously. I was so bitter about the situation and needed an outlet. I said something foolish. I never wanted this result."

"What... what are you saying, Annie?" Lady Kate clutched Mary's arm.

I closed the gap between me and Annie, Lord Albert hovering close, the tension in the air ramping almost to breaking point. "The result you got was convincing Celeste to kill her dad for you."

# Chapter 22

Annie and Celeste glared at each other. Neither of them spoke or blinked.

"Celeste, say something." Mary was pale as she stared at her daughter. "You aren't involved, are you?"

Celeste's lips thinned, and she tore her gaze from Annie's face. "She said the nuts wouldn't kill him, and it was just for fun. Daddy would go red and his lips would swell, so he looked like an ugly fish. Annie said she'd done the research, and a few wouldn't be fatal. I wanted to get him back for not buying me the horse and the apartment."

Annie turned away from Celeste. "Lady Kate, Lady Mary, you know what Celeste is like. She talks to imaginary friends. She's making this up, just like she does so many things."

"You said you thought it was cute I had imaginary friends," Celeste said. "But they're not imaginary. I see them."

"Why?" Mary said, her voice barely a whisper. "What did your father do to you to make you want to kill him?"

"I already said I didn't want him dead." Celeste's cheeks were blotchy with color. "But he wouldn't buy me what I wanted. And he even laughed when I demanded a new car."

"Celeste! The last time you drove a car, you wrote it off," Mary said. "I can't believe what you're saying. You really did this?"

"Daddy was stopping me from being free. I want to live on my own. I'm sick of always been watched and told what to do." Celeste jabbed a finger at Annie. "She said we could move in together and be roommates. Annie said she'd take care of me and be my best friend."

All eyes turned to Annie, who was glowering at Celeste.

"Is this true?" Lady Kate said.

Annie raised her hands. "Of course not. Celeste made a mistake. It wouldn't be the first time. I like her and want to look after her the same as all of you. It's what a loyal employee does. She got things confused in her head."

"I saw them," Julian said quietly.

"When?" Lady Kate turned to her son. "What were they doing?"

His nervous gaze shot to me, and I nodded, hoping he'd be reassured that he could speak without being judged. "Celeste and Annie had been acting weird all day, and they left the house together. I wanted to know what they were up to, so I followed them. They... bought a bag of nuts."

"Liar! Don't listen to him. He's too doped up on anti-crazy pills to be useful to anyone," Celeste said. "That's another reason I want out of here. I'm sick of my annoying little brother hanging around and pretending he can see ghosts, too. It's pathetic."

"Celeste, you can't keep talking like this is one of your fantasies," Mary said. "You'll get in trouble. Admit this is a silly game, and everyone will forget about it. You had nothing to do with what happened to your father."

"I don't think we can forget," I said.

Mary raised a trembling hand to her mouth. "But... I don't want to believe it. She can't be telling the truth."

"No one ever listens to me when I tell them about ghosts. Annie believes me." Celeste shoved her hands into her hair and tugged it. "At least, I thought she did. Now, everything has gone wrong. Daddy didn't just get fat lips and look silly. He died. That was never supposed to happen."

"Annie told you to keep quiet about what you'd planned to do to Lord Albert?" I said.

Celeste's eyes narrowed to tiny slits. "She did. She told me not to say anything, and we'd soon be out of here. And you're right about her foot. Annie faked the injury." She marched over and kicked Annie's cast. "I hate you. This is your fault."

Annie backed away and licked her lips. "Stupid girl. I said only three nuts. You put half the bag into Lord Albert's meal. There was nothing I could do but watch you screw everything up. If you'd kept control, no one would have known. We could have left together."

"You were never taking me with you. I thought you liked me!" Celeste kicked her again.

Annie had the decency to look ashamed, but indignation still glinted in her eyes. "Emma would always have been under suspicion over what happened. We would have gotten away with it, if you'd just kept quiet."

"Neither of you will get away with anything." I had my phone out and was already calling the police.

Celeste shoved Annie, and she toppled over. She lost her balance as her booted foot made her unsteady and hit the carpeted floor. Celeste went to kick Annie again, but Mary dashed over and pulled her daughter away.

"Enough! No more lies. Celeste, I'm so ashamed of you. Your own father. How could you?" Mary gripped Celeste's arms.

Celeste stared at her mom, then at Annie, and burst into tears.

I connected with the police and informed them about what I'd uncovered, my hands shaking as I tried to stay calm. I'd been fooled by Celeste. I never realized she was so unstable. All this time, I'd been worried about Julian being a danger to other people, when Celeste was the one we should have kept an eye on.

Helen poked her head around the bedroom door. "I wondered where everyone was. Have I missed out on anything important?"

"I still can't believe it. I turn my back for five minutes, and you solve the mystery." Helen stood behind me as she curled my hair.

I looked at her in the reflection of the bedroom mirror. "It's hardly my fault. You keep disappearing. Although I'm not sure I'd have ever figured out Celeste was involved if Julian hadn't spoken up about seeing her buying nuts with Annie."

"And you have Annie to thank, too, since she decided she wasn't going down for Lord Albert's murder alone." Helen twirled a strand of my hair around the hot tongs. "Do you think she liked Celeste, or was she using her?"

"Annie saw an opportunity for revenge and exploited a vulnerable young woman. She manipulated Celeste into being an accomplice and doing her dirty work for her. Annie preyed on her weakness and desire to escape and have someone not judge her."

After the police had taken Celeste and Annie in for questioning, I'd brought Helen up to speed about the discoveries I found and the revelations revealed in Annie's room. And although she'd been interested, she'd been distracted the whole time I'd talked. Something was still off with her, but I couldn't put my finger on it. Her energy had a nervous spike to it, and she kept talking too quickly.

"I'm glad it's over. Now we can focus on all the fun." She finished curling my hair and stepped back. "That looks amazing."

"Thanks. I still don't think we should go out tonight, though. The family is in shock. We should be here to support them."

"They won't want outsiders hanging around. Besides, everything is in hand. The police have Celeste and Annie, Mary and Lady Kate have formed a friendship and are helping each other, and Julian's with them. We should let them have their family time. They've got a lot to work through."

"Maybe we won't have jobs tomorrow. Lady Kate may think hosting the Winter Wonderland Gala isn't appropriate. After all, her step-daughter helped murder her husband."

"If that's the decision she makes, we'll accept it. That's out of our hands," Helen said. "But we deserve a break. This has been a stressful few days. We came here expecting to plan a party and instead got involved in a murder mystery. Again."

"Some things never change." I smiled at her.

"And the restaurant I booked for us sounds amazing. They're having a six-course Christmas tasting menu. Three of the courses are dessert."

I laughed. "I'm sold. But I want to check in on the family before we go, just in case they're having a hard time coming to terms with everything that's happened."

"If you insist. But we don't have much time. We can't miss our slot."

"Do we need to be so dressed up?" I preferred office clothes or practical gear to walk Flipper in, but Helen had insisted on not only styling my hair and doing my make-up, but had picked me a pretty pale pink dress with a high waistline. She'd said it was from her closet, but I'd never seen it before, and it was a perfect fit for me.

"Yes! Now come on, hurry!" Helen wore a beautiful dress in a deep red tone, her blonde curls piled up on her head. She looked like Santa's dream woman.

We hurried down the stairs, Flipper already waiting at the bottom as if he knew we were going out. There was a knock on the front door, and I opened it to find Emma outside, clutching her purse.

"I don't mean to intrude, but I heard about Annie and Celeste. I wanted to see if there was anything I could do to help the family." Her gaze shifted over my shoulder. "Do you think they could do with some support?"

"Your timing is perfect," Helen said. "And no one's eaten yet. Go in and see how they're doing. They'll appreciate a friendly face."

Emma remained on the step. "I don't want to get in the way. And I know I'm not a member of the family, but I worked here for so long, I felt I had to come. Mary must be feeling terrible. And I can't believe Celeste was involved. Oh dear, this was a mistake. I should go. They'll think I'm interfering."

"Emma, is that you?" Lady Kate stepped out of a nearby room and approached the front door.

Emma gave a quick nod. "Sorry. I can leave if you don't want me here. It's just that—"

"You're very welcome. And I owe you an apology." Lady Kate stopped at the open door. "All this time, I've been persecuting you. Please, come in. There's a lot we need to talk about. And perhaps, if you'd consider coming back, we'd appreciate having someone we can trust close by at this difficult time."

Emma's eyes glazed with tears. "Oh! Well, I'd like that. I've missed the place."

"And I'll pay you what I owe you. With a Christmas bonus, of course." Lady Kate's expression was full of shame. "I didn't want to believe a member of the family killed Albert. But when Lorna and Helen started asking questions, the secrets came out, and I must accept the truth of the situation. You're an innocent woman. I'll make sure everyone knows that."

"That's... Thank you. And of course, it was the right thing to do, defending your family." Emma bustled in, her cheeks flushed with surprised delight. She stopped and gently patted Lady Kate's arm. "Why don't I make us something to eat? We can sit down and sort things out, just like old times. And we have a Christmas menu to finalize. Oh, my. There's so much to do!"

"I'd like that. Welcome home, Emma." Lady Kate waited until Emma had gone into the kitchen before looking at us, her expression softening. "You both look lovely."

"Are you sure it's okay if we go out?" I said. "We can cancel the reservation. Helen surprised me with the plan at the last minute."

Lady Kate glanced at Helen and smiled. "This is one reservation you won't want to miss. I hope you have a wonderful night. And don't worry about coming back late. I doubt any of us will get much sleep as we digest our situation."

"It's just dinner," I said. "We'll be back by nine."

"No, we won't," Helen said. "We're making a night of it. And thank you, Lady Kate. We plan to have an amazing evening. It'll be unforgettable."

"Is the food really that good?" I said.

Helen chuckled. "Out of this world."

"And we can discuss the gala in the morning," Lady Kate said, "but having talked to Mary, she thinks it should go ahead. Of course, she's devastated over what Celeste did, but we're dealing with things. Christmas can't be canceled because of our sad discovery."

"That's good news. It'll give you something to look forward to." I glanced over her shoulder to see Lord Albert drifting around.

"I'm glad it's over, and we know the truth. Although I'm in shock over Annie's betrayal. It was cruel of her to delude Celeste. But at least this horrible chapter is at an end. We'll close the door and look toward a positive future. Starting with the Winter Wonderland Gala."

I wanted to say more, but Helen was nudging me out the door. After a quick goodbye, we hurried outside. Helen brought the car around, and we jumped in, Flipper getting in the back seat, before we zoomed away.

"Where's Milly?" I said. "If this place lets Flipper in, she'll be no trouble."

"Oh, I... sent her ahead."

"Ahead? You left her at the restaurant on her own?"

"Something like that. It'll all make sense soon."

"I doubt that." Very little of Helen's recent behavior made sense to me. I hoped it was just a blip and order would soon be restored.

After ten minutes of driving with Christmas carols floating out of the car stereo, I noticed we weren't heading into town. "Isn't this the way to the animal sanctuary?"

"Is it?" Helen glanced around. "You know me, I'm terrible at directions."

"You're usually pretty good at finding places. I'm sure this is the way to the sanctuary, though."

"Hmmm. I must be having an off day. Let's keep going. Maybe this is a shortcut."

Within a couple of minutes, we turned down the lane that led directly to the animal sanctuary.

I shifted in my seat so I could look at Helen. "What's going on?"

She grinned and jigged up and down in her seat. "I've been bursting to tell you. I never thought I'd be able to keep this a secret from you."

"Has this got to do with your new puppy? I thought Zach was helping with that. We can't take the pup to a fancy restaurant. It would be chaos."

"No. This has nothing to do with my new arrival."

"Gunner hasn't found out and said he doesn't want the pup, has he? They are a huge commitment, but I'm sure you can talk him around."

"Absolutely not. That little pup is coming home with us, even if Gunner objects. Which he won't. But... Well, you'll soon see." Helen pulled the car into the parking lot, and we all climbed out.

I was surprised to see the place lit up with strings of beautiful fairy lights over the doorway, making it look like a magical winter grotto. A path had been cleared through the snow, leading to a set of large double doors. "Are we going inside? They serve food here?"

"We are. Just a second." Helen opened the trunk. She called over Flipper, and he sat beside her as she put a red bowtie around his neck.

"What are you doing to Flipper? And why do we have to dress up to go in the animal sanctuary?"

There was a glint of mischief in Helen's eyes as she looked at me. "You missed all the clues. And I'm so glad you did. Although I reckon you'd have figured it out if Lord Albert's murder hadn't distracted you. This is one occasion when I'm glad you had a murder to solve."

"You're happy someone died?"

"No! But it kept you from solving this mystery."

"What mystery are you talking about?"

The door to the animal sanctuary opened, and my eyes widened as Zach stood there in a smart black suit and tie. He shifted from foot to foot then grinned and strode over.

"What are you doing here?" I looked him up and down. "And why are you dressed like that?"

Helen cleared her throat, and I turned to look at her. She held out a beautiful bouquet of red and pink roses. She waved them at me. "These are for you. And if you've not figured out the mystery based on this huge clue, you'll have to retire from sleuthing."

I stared at Zach, then the flowers, then Flipper, who sat proudly in his red bowtie.

Zach caught hold of my elbow. "I know you don't like surprises, but—"

"This is a wedding. Is it our wedding?" I blurted out.

Helen laughed. "Finally! Of course, this is your wedding."

"I don't understand. How? Why? And what's with all the secrecy?"

Zach kissed my cheek. "You look beautiful. And, in case I need to remind you, you hate change. And you're stubborn. I've been trying to get a date out of you for our wedding for ages. Every time I brought up the subject, you said there was no rush. But I want to marry you, Lorna Shadow. More than anything else in this world."

"So you tricked me into attending my own wedding?" I had so many emotions whirling through me, I didn't know which one to land on first. The main one was shock, but there was also a flicker of delight. I was about to marry Zach.

Helen pinched my arm. "It's not a trick. Zach loves you, and you love him. You're already engaged, and you live together. I've been talking to Zach for a while, trying to find a way to give you a shove, so you would set a date. Then we visited the animal sanctuary. They had a last minute wedding cancellation, and that got me thinking..."

"Wait! The secret calls and messages, and you vanishing all the time. You were planning the wedding?" I said.

"Yes! It seemed perfect for you and Zach to take this slot. So I got in touch with the wedding planner, and we had everything switched into your names, with Zach's approval, of course. The food, the music, and I even got some guests for the meal afterward. Although, since it was so last-minute, it's only going to be small. And only me, Gunner, and the fur babies will be at the ceremony. But we'll make up for that after Christmas with a huge party. And I plan on inviting everyone."

I held up my hands. "Wait! I need a minute to process." I looked at the animal sanctuary, lit up and sparkling. I wasn't a traditionalist when it came to marriage and had always wanted something simple, surrounded by the people and things I loved the most. And it was all right here. I thought of Helen like a sister, although an annoying sister who did things behind my back without telling me. But Zach was here, and I'd just spotted Gunner grinning wildly at me, Milly in his arms and Jessie sitting beside him. Flipper was also here, my most beloved fur baby. Everyone I cared about most would see me marry the man I loved. And although it was scary, and Zach was right, change didn't come easy to me, this felt perfect.

Zach placed an arm around my waist. "When Helen suggested it, I wasn't sure. But everything made sense. It seemed to fit just right. But if you don't want to do it—"

"I do. Let's get married. This is exactly what I'd have planned." I kissed his cheek. "Admittedly, I'd have liked to have been involved in the planning." I shot a half-hearted glare at Helen, but then laughed at the enormous smile on her face.

"I knew this would be ideal for you and Zach. It's intimate and surrounded by your favorite things.

Fate threw us this opportunity, and you were so busy at work and dealing with Lord Albert that you missed it. Fortunately, you have an amazing best friend, and she'll never let you down."

"Remind me to thank that friend with a big gift at Christmas."

"Oh, I will. And you're welcome. Now, how about we go get you married?"

I sucked in a deep breath and looked at Zach. "Are we really doing this?"

"If you'll have me, I can't think of anything else I'd rather do."

Helen hurried ahead and spoke to Gunner. Zach walked me to the door then kissed the back of my hand. "No second thoughts?"

"I've hardly had time for first thoughts." A laugh of pure delight shot out of me. "I can't believe it. We're getting married."

"At last. I finally get to have you all to myself."

I touched his cheek. "You wonderful man. You've always had me. Of course, you'll always be sharing me with Flipper. And Helen."

"I know the deal. And I'm all in."

Helen hurried back. "Zach, you need to get in position."

Zach winked at me. "See you in a minute." He hurried off.

"I don't know whether to shake you or kiss you," I said to Helen.

"No punishment or thanks required." She grabbed my free hand, tears in her eyes. "Lorna, you're always thinking about other people and putting their needs first. I decided you needed to be made number one, even if it's just for one night. Your happiness comes first."

Tears flooded my eyes. "You made this dress?"

"I did. I stayed up late for several nights after you'd gone to sleep to get it done. And I even found time to bake you and Zach an amazing cake. It doesn't have loads of tiers, but it'll taste incredible."

"Does anyone else know?"

"Lady Kate and Julian. I had to tell them when they caught me carrying cake tins to my room. They fully support the plan, and Lady Kate was delighted something positive was happening after experiencing so much sadness."

"Have I ever told you, you're the best friend a woman could ever need?"

"Even though I don't come with fur?"

"I'll even overlook that flaw." I hugged her tight. "Thank you. This is wonderful."

"And so are you." Helen smoothed my hair. "We both are. So, how about it?"

My gaze shifted as a shimmer appeared, and Lord Albert materialized. "Um... Just give me a minute."

"Lorna! You're about to get married to the love of your life."

"Wait for me at the entrance. I want to say goodbye to Lord Albert."

"You have thirty seconds." Helen glared around the parking lot. "Lord Albert, do not delay this crucially important event."

He smiled at me and gave me a thumbs-up as Helen hurried away.

"I hope you're okay after learning what happened," I said. "Celeste seems troubled, but

I'm sure she'll get the help she needs. And I truly hope Annie goes away for a long time for deceiving everyone."

He nodded then lifted his chin toward the animal sanctuary.

"I know. Change is coming for us all, including you. Are you ready to move on now?"

He nodded, leaned forward, and brushed an icy kiss across my cheek. Then he faded out of sight with a wistful smile on his face.

"Lorna, get a move on. You're about to get married," Helen called from the doorway.

I was just turning to her when Julian appeared around the side of the animal sanctuary and hurried toward me through the snow.

"Sorry to interrupt. I know you're doing something important, but I didn't want to miss you."

My eyebrows flashed up. "Is everything okay? Shouldn't you be with your family?"

He grinned. "I needed a breather from the talking and hand wringing. Mom let me out for an hour. And I'm better than okay."

Julian looked happier than I'd ever seen him. "I'm glad to hear that. You're not upset about Celeste and Annie being arrested?"

He tilted his head from side to side. "More like relieved. And glad I had nothing to do with it. I've promised my family I won't mess with my medication anymore. And... if you're willing, I could do with a ghost mentor for when things get tricky."

"You've got it. And when I leave, we'll stay in touch online."

"Great. So…" His grin widened. "I took your advice and came here with dad. We found one."

"One what?"

"A pup like Flipper. He could see dad's ghost. And the puppy likes me. He's perfect."

I pressed a hand against my chest. "Julian, that's wonderful news."

"I just need to convince Mom we can adopt him, but I reckon she'll want me to have a friend. And if he helps me with the ghosts, she'll support it. Do you want to see him? He's in the cab."

"No!" Helen strode over. "Puppies later. Lorna is about to get married. No more delays."

I really did want to see the pup, but I also had the man of my dreams to unite with and make my husband. "Um…"

"Lorna Shadow!" Helen pursed her lips. "Don't you dare."

"Wait right here." Julian dashed off, sliding across the snow in his haste to get the puppy.

"You're late for your wedding! You don't have time to coo over a puppy."

"Helen, it's a puppy. A pup that'll save Julian from the ghosts. And Zach is a dog lover. He'll completely understand a short delay in the name of a fur baby."

She grumbled under her breath, but her complaints ceased as Julian ran back with a fluffy ginger puppy in his arms. "Oh! He's like mine. They must be brothers."

"He's adorable," I said.

"And he was amazing with Dad's ghost," Julian said. "I guess I won't see Dad anymore, will I? Has he gone?"

"He crossed over a minute ago. His mystery is solved, so he can move on knowing you're safe and happy. This little guy will be amazing for you. Just what you need."

Julian hugged the pup, who was trying to lick his chin. "He will. I've got to go get him in the warmth. Have a great wedding." He turned and raced back to the car.

I took another deep breath and turned to Helen. "Everything's worked out perfectly."

"It has. And since Lord Albert has gone, you have nothing stopping you from walking along the aisle." She arched an eyebrow. "Unless you've changed your mind."

"Oh, no. I'm all in."

"Wait until you see your wedding cake. It's definitely worth getting married for."

I laughed. "Since you made it, I've no doubt. Go! I'll walk in with Flipper."

Helen kissed my cheek and squeaked. "This is so exciting. Head through the doors in front of you and be prepared to enter a wedding winter wonderland." She hurried away.

I waited with Flipper for a moment, giving myself a chance to catch my breath and not miss a second of this incredible event.

As I reached the door, I nodded and smiled at several center volunteers holding animals and grinning as they watched me walk toward my happily ever after.

My gaze went to the window as snow started gently drifting down, and I took my first step toward married life. Flipper walked alongside me, his tail wagging as he looked resplendent in his red bowtie.

My breath caught as I took in the explosion of white and glitter in the small ceremony room. This was so Helen. Lights shimmered across the ceiling, candles lit the room with a warm, cozy glow, and wild winter heather and gorse filled all the spaces.

I nodded at the celebrant as I reached Zach, took his hand, and smiled into his warm, open face.

He leaned down, and his mouth brushed my ear. "Merry Christmas, my new wife."

I brushed my cheek against his. "This'll be a perfect Christmas for everyone. Thanks for waiting for me."

"Always. And there'll be many more to come."

My gaze shifted to Helen and Gunner, who stood with Milly, Jessie, Flipper, and a squirming bundle of ginger fluff, and smiled so broadly my cheeks hurt.

My family was a little messy, many of them covered in fur, all of them adorable, and I wouldn't change a single thing about them. They often surprised and annoyed me, but most of all, they made my life complete.

I squeezed Zach's hand. "So, what are we waiting for? Let's get married."

If you haven't tried the rest of the Lorna Shadow mysteries (there are 12 more books) you can enjoy a bumper edition of the first six stories in a single set. The boxed set features:

**Ghostly Manners** - A new job. A haunted house. A ghost with a problem
**Ghostly Secrets** - A troubled ghost. A house full of suspects, and a mystery that must be solved
**Ghostly Games** - An unsolved disappearance. Ghostly laughter. An ectoplasmic experience
**Ghostly Affairs** - A house full of secrets. Two restless ghosts. A murder mystery to solve
**Ghostly Business** - A haunted castle full of suspects and an eccentric ghost who refuses to rest
**Ghostly Rules** - Dark deeds. Missing gold. A ghost with twenty-five million secrets

Available on Amazon

# About Author

K.E. O'Connor (Karen) is a cozy mystery author living in the beautiful British countryside. She loves all things mystery, animals, and cake. When she's not writing, she volunteers at a local animal sanctuary, reads a ton of books, binge-watches mystery series, and dreams about living somewhere warmer.

If you'd like to be one of the first to know when a new book comes out, sign up for her newsletter. Not only will you get fun news and updates on books every week, you'll also get an exclusive **FREE** Lorna Shadow novella – Ghostly Fowl.

**Newsletter:**
www.subscribepage.com/cozymysteries
**Website:**
www.keoconnor.com/writing
**Facebook:**
www.facebook.com/keoconnorauthor

# Also By

Other books in the Lorna Shadow series:

Ghostly Manners
Ghostly Secrets
Ghostly Games
Ghostly Affairs
Ghostly Business
Ghostly Rules
Ghostly Waves
Ghostly Play
Ghostly Proposal
Ghostly Vows
Ghostly Fright
Ghostly Hunt
Ghostly Surprises